THE 400 POUND SPY

The 400 Pound Spy

Michael Downey

To My Wife, Melinda

Chapter 1

Peter Smith sat down at a table at the Tenth Man, a sports themed bar connected to his hotel in Phoenix. There was a group of 8-10 young men spread out over three tables watching an Arizona Diamondbacks baseball game on a big screen TV. They seemed to be enjoying the drinks as much as the game, and the better the Diamondbacks performed, the louder the group got. Peter Smith sat down at a table away from the revelers. On the wall above him was a framed, autographed photo of Kurt Warner, the retired Hall of Fame quarterback who played with the Arizona Cardinals. His red number 13 jersey hung beneath the photo and was also signed.

A young woman wearing a red and yellow Arizona State University t-shirt was serving drinks at a nearby table. The back of her shirt said JEN. She approached Peter Smith's table to take his order.

"Hi, I'm Jen. What can I get you?"
Before Peter Smith could answer, the baseball fans cheered loudly.

"What are they having?"

"They're all drinking our special-- the Diamondback Venom."

"Sounds interesting. What's in it?"

"It's got rum..." The crowd cheered again, drowning her out.

"Sounds good," he said, not really knowing what else was in the drink but rum.

"Do you want that in a souvenir cup for a dollar

more?"

"Sure. It will remind me of you."

Jen eyed him for a second after that remark. It looked as if she was wondering if she should smile or roll her eyes. She compromised and left with no reaction.

Peter Smith continued to survey the room. He spotted a woman coming in his direction. She was about 5'8" although it was hard to tell because she was hunched over. She may have been attractive, but she had so much makeup on that it was hard to tell exactly what she looked like, and her long brown hair also obscured her face. She wore a baggy Arizona State sweatshirt with jeans, both hiding her figure. The only distinguishing characteristic was her gait. She stumbled as she walked as if she had been having too much of a good time. She was holding a glass of what was likely Diamondback Venom. The crowd cheered, and she cheered belatedly with no idea what was happening on the screen.

She stopped, took out her lipstick and applied it liberally then used a napkin to moderate it some. She steadied herself and once again began walking his way. She was perhaps moving too quickly for her condition and nearly stumbled into Peter Smith's lap. She caught herself and placed her drink on the table in front of him and steadied herself. Their eyes met for a moment, and then she picked up her drink and walked on.

Peter Smith recognized those green eyes. Underneath the make-up and the wig and the phony drunk act was a friend. He looked down at the table, and where her drink had been, was a napkin. It contained a message. Written in red lipstick was a circle with a cross inside. Peter Smith recognized the crimson cross. He was in danger.

Jen arrived a few seconds later with his venom. He laid some cash on the table and looked around. He did not know what to expect. Was someone outside the bar waiting for him? Were they in his hotel room now? He raised the venom to his lips but stopped short of taking a drink. Fortunately, he was trained to be prepared for something like this. Before leaving for the bar, he grabbed his duffel bag packed with twenty thousand dollars, a change of clothes and a couple of different ID's. The first one was Jean St. Sebastian. He had used it a few times when working in Europe. The other was Xavier Carnahaha. This one was off the books. He had a forger in Sydney create it for him a few years earlier. He had a driver's license and passport and even a library card. Xavier Carnahaha was a reader. No one knew about this identity except for his friend and fellow agent Candace Kane. Peter Smith picked up his duffel bag, got up from the table and walked out of the bar. An hour later Xavier Carnahaha checked in at the Holiday Inn.

Chapter 2

The big man placed a silencer on his Lugar before knocking on the hotel room door. There was no answer. He looked down the hall for witnesses. The hall was quiet. He knocked again and said, "Hotel security." Still no answer. He pocketed his pistol and took out a thin piece of metal sometimes referred to as a "slim jim." After a few seconds, he jimmied the lock and let himself in. He turned on a light and surveyed the room. There were two twin beds. Both were made up with matching paisley comforters. An open suitcase sat on one. The Russian looked through the clothes in the suitcase. There was nothing there particularly interesting. To an outsider, it would look like it belonged to an average traveler on vacation. But the Russian knew better. A white envelope on the dresser caught his eye. He picked it up and pulled out an airplane ticket. It was for the next morning-- Phoenix to Kahului, Seat 7B, and the name on the ticket was Peter Smith.

"I don't believe you'll be making that flight, Peter Smith."

The Russian snickered. After a few seconds, the laugh turned into a cough. The big man placed his gun on a table next to an office chair then he wedged himself into the chair. He picked up the gun and rubbed his hand up and down the barrel.

"Oh yes, Peter Smith, there will be no Hawaiian vacation for you."

He sat for a few seconds and then realized he had not shut off the light. He wiggled out of the chair, shut off the light and then once again forced himself upon the office chair. He sat in the hotel room in the dark and waited.

After an hour, the Russian got bored and tired and hungry. Sitting in the dark waiting to put a bullet in the enemy wasn't all it was cracked up to be. The chair was uncomfortable.

"These hotels need bigger chairs."

His thoughts turned to Peter Smith.

"Where is this American fool? He's probably with some woman he met at the bar. American agents are weak with their liquor and their women. The Russians are superior in every way."

He started to get discouraged. There was no telling when the American would return. He took out the Burger King coupon he had in his pocket – buy one whooper get one free. His stomach growled. Killing Peter Smith would have to wait. The Russian freed himself from the chair.

"I'll see you on the plane tomorrow, Peter Smith. Enjoy your women tonight."

The Russian left the hotel room and drove to Burger King.

Chapter 3

Donald "Duke" Duckworth grimaced as he approached the counter at Gate A25 in Phoenix's Sky Harbor International Airport. He and his wife Daisy had arrived in Phoenix from St. Louis, the first leg on what was supposed to be their dream vacation to Hawaii. He and Daisy had been married 25 years, and they had planned long ago to spend their silver anniversary in Hawaii.

They were practically penniless the day they went to the courthouse to be married. They spent their honeymoon in The Little Motel in Sedalia, Missouri, and went to a concert at the Missouri State Fair courtesy of his friend Marco who got them free tickets through the radio station where he worked. Johnny Boy Sims was playing. Neither Duke nor Daisy were fans of Johnny Boy, but it was their honeymoon, so it would be the best concert ever and one they would always remember. His song, Alligator Love and Crocodile Kisses became their new favorite song. So, while it wasn't exactly the perfect honeymoon, it did have its moments. The couple was determined to make the 25th anniversary trip everything the honeymoon was not.

Duke planned the trip through an online travel agent. He spent hours working on the details. He found the perfect resort-- the Isle of Lahaina on Maui. It certainly would be a step up from The Little Motel. The online description promised great views of the Pacific Ocean and of Haleakala-- the volcano on the island. The Little Motel had a view of the Highway

50/65 interchange.

Finding a flight from Missouri to Hawaii was a little tricky. There were no direct flights except maybe with the B2 Bombers that were stationed at Whiteman Air Force Base in Central Missouri. But they didn't really take passengers, and even if they did, it was probably not a flight that a vacationing couple would want to be on. Duke finally settled on a St. Louis to Phoenix to Maui itinerary. It was relatively short-- only eleven hours of travel time-- and it would get them to the island in the afternoon. He even purchased tickets on a shuttle to the hotel. He had worked out all of the details...well, almost. It wasn't until they picked up their boarding passes in Phoenix when the couple realized they would not be sitting next to each other on the six-hour flight. In fact, they would be rows apart-- not a good way to begin the trip of their dreams. So, Duke approached the agent at the gate just before boarding began.

"Can I help you?"

Duke smiled at the woman across the counter and glanced at her name tag. He decided to turn on the charm.

"Hi Rebecca. That's a beautiful name. A beautiful name for a beautiful woman."

The airline worker seemed unmoved by the complement.

"What can I do for you?"

"My wife and I don't have seats together. Is there any way we could make a little change?"

Rebecca pulled up the flight on her monitor.

"Let's see. The flight is full. I'm afraid you're out of luck."

"Oh, come on, Becky. Is it OK if I call you Becky?"

"No."

"Right, Rebecca, like Sunnybrook Farm."

"Huh?"

"Anyway, Rebecca, sweet Rebecca, you have to help me out here. It's our second honeymoon, and we can't spend the next six hours apart, or I might spend the next six nights on the couch. You know what I mean?"

He stiffly smiled.

Rebecca hit a couple more keys.

"You might be in luck. The passenger in the seat next to your wife has not checked in yet. You can try sitting in his seat, and if he doesn't show up, you'll be fine."

"Becky, you're my hero. Seriously, you're the best. I'd hug you if I could."

"That's quite all right. You folks have a nice trip."

Chapter 4

Candace Kane thought she would be promoted to Head of Linguistics. She spoke ten languages and had mastered dozens of dialects. But she was passed over in favor of Winston Salem who could barely speak his native tongue. Salem was also a pig. He called her Candy, and whenever he saw her, he would say, "There she is, my little handy dandy Candy Kane. Come on over and give me a little sweetness." He had tried to kiss her more than once, but she was just as good at fighting off the letches as she was the Russians.

Winston Salem had never been in a position of responsibility, but the executive team of the Shop saw something in him, and he was promoted. Candace knew her options were limited. She was part of a secret espionage agency. They didn't exactly have an HR office she could complain to. Even if there were someone to complain to, what would be the outcome? Would they call in all the spies and assassins for a workshop on sexual harassment?

While she was pondering her options, she got a call from Martin Martinson, Chief of Operations. He wanted to see her right away.

"I need you to go to Maui," he said as she walked into his office.

"Maui, OK, what's going on?"

"It's the Pit. There up to something there. We have deployed Peter Smith, but we...I...he might need some support on the ground there."

"OK, where is he now?"

"He's flying out of Phoenix in the morning."

"OK."

"He doesn't know you're going. No one knows."

"What aren't you telling me, Chief."

"We have a problem. We intercepted this phone call an hour ago."

Martinson played the recording. The man's voice was purposely distorted, but the message was perfectly clear.

"It's me. I'm sending you Peter Smith's file. There is no photo available…I don't know, the guy doesn't like his picture taken. Some people are like that…Are you going to kill him tonight?... Good. When can I expect my money?... OK, but make it cash and not those filthy rubles."

"Where did this call originate from?"

"The conference room."

"Our conference room?"

"We have a traitor. For now, you are the only one I can trust."

"Got it."

Candace left immediately for Phoenix. Later that evening at the Tenth Man, she would warn Peter Smith with the crimson cross.

Chapter 5

Feyodor Arbackle. Jr. was on his first mission for the Pit, an international criminal organization operated by Russian mobsters with ties to the government. It had nearly been put out of business just a few years earlier. Their top operatives had either been captured or killed, but it was making a comeback thanks to the international heroin trade. With the absence of experienced field agents, the organization was now relying on eager staff who had always wanted to be agents but who had been passed over for various reasons. Many of them had worked at The Pit headquarters reading maps, studying languages, and looking for online bargains. They weren't very good agents, but they were great at finding good Groupon offers. The new Pit had to keep an eye on the budget.

Arbackle was the son of one of the masterminds of the Pit. But he was not a favorite son. His father wasn't even certain the large child was his, and he refused to call him by his name. He didn't even call him Junior or FJ. No, Feyordor Arbackle called his son "Fatty." The child's mother, a singer who performed a Madonna tribute act, caught Arbackle's eye one night in Moscow. She sang "Express Yourself," and he did. The result was Feyordor Arbackle Jr. His mother convinced the senior Arbackle to give his son a low-level job with the criminal organization. His specialty was finding cheap buffets and buy-one-get-one-free specials for the agents in the field. Judging by his size, he was very good at his research. He had always wanted to be a field agent, and with the diminished talent at the Pit, he finally got his opportunity.

He hated to be called Fatty. But that is how they knew him at The Pit thanks to his father. It was always, "Morning, Fatty…How's it going, Fatty…Hey Fatty, find me a good deal in Seattle." That was one of the reasons why he was glad to leave the headquarters and become a field agent. He could change his name. No longer would he be known as Fatty Arbackle. He would become Samson Betters. That is the name he told the forgers at headquarters he wanted. He also told them he wanted to come from a typical American town, so that he would fit it. He stuck a pin in the middle of a map of the United States, and it landed on a little town called Sedalia, Missouri. Samson loved it. It rolled off his tongue. "Hi, I'm Samson from Sedalia." It would be perfect. He looked it up on Wikipedia and learned a few facts about it, but he didn't feel the need to know too much. America was a big country, and the chances of finding someone who knew anything about the small Missouri town in Hawaii would be remote. Besides, he was going undercover as a minister. No one would question a minister.

As part of his mission, he had one very important task he needed to complete—kill Peter Smith. He had missed him at his hotel room, but he would get him on the plane. Peter Smith must die.

Chapter 6

Daisy and Duke Duckworth found their adjoining seats on the plane. Daisy had the window seat, and Duke was in the middle as long as the actual ticket holder didn't show up.

"How long is the flight?" Daisy took out her tablet loaded up with books she had downloaded.

"Six hours to paradise and our second honeymoon." Then after a slight pause, "Alligator love…"

Daisy did not respond. He repeated, "Alligator love…"

"And Crocodile kisses…"

"Happy anniver…"

"Is this Row 7, Seat C?"

Duke looked up to see a very large man hovering over the seat next to him. He was at least 6'5" and Duke figured he weighed 400 pounds.

"Yes, it is."

Duke watched in wonder as the large man wedged himself into his seat. He thought the guy was going to need a shoehorn. He moved and shifted and inhaled and exhaled trying desperately to fit in the seat. Then came the seat belt. With great effort, he convinced it to snap in place over him. Duke felt sympathy for the little strap. It was going to earn its money today.

The man could not sit still. With his seat belt fastened, he was like a trapped whale, as he flailed about trying to make himself a little less uncomfortable. Every time he moved, both Duke's and Daisy's seats moved too. Duke had a vision of all three seats breaking off as the man stood up. He and Daisy would be swinging around as the giant twisted and shook.

"Hey, do you mind if I put the arm down?"

He lowered the arm between them without waiting for a response. Duke scooted closer to Daisy as the big man's girth oozed into his seat. He leaned over towards Duke.

"Sorry, I'm so big. I have been all my life. I was 11 pounds when I was born."

"Wow."

Duke thought the man had come a long way from 11 pounds.

"Eleven pounds!"

The woman behind Duke spoke.

"Your poor mother. Bless her heart."

"Yeah, I was always bigger than all the other kids, even some of the adults."

"Well, bless your heart."

"Yeah, poor him. What about the rest of us?" Duke thought as he scooted closer to Daisy to avoid coming in contact with the large man.

"My sister had a ten-pound girl, and she has had problems all her life," the woman behind Duke chimed in.

"That's a shame."

"The doctors in Kentucky just don't know what to do with her."

"Kentucky, huh?"

"Yeah, where are you all from?"

"Missouri."

Duke suddenly got interested in the conversation.

"Where are you from?"

"Missouri."

"We're from Missouri too."

Duke nudged Daisy. She kept her eyes on the tablet. The big man's eyes narrowed when Duke said this.

"Where do you live?"

"It's a little town called Sedalia. It's in Pettis County. Population 21,836."

"Oh, we know all about Sedalia. We spent our honeymoon there."

"I preach at a little church in Sedalia."

"We're from Columbia. We both work at Mizzou."

Duke pointed to the black and gold hat he was wearing that said MIZZOU.

"Oh yeah, the Missouri Zoo? Right?"

The conversation seemed to make the man uncomfortable.

"What? No. Mizzou. Mizzou. The University of Missouri."

"Oh yeah, up by St. Louis."

Duke didn't answer. Columbia was nowhere near St. Louis. Why was this man lying about being from Missouri?

The flight attendant began the pre-flight announcements, and the conversation between the passengers ceased. Duke was certain the flight to paradise was going to be hell, but the owner of the seat didn't show up, so as least he would be sitting next to his wife.

Chapter 7

Peter Smith did not show up to the Phoenix airport for his flight. He was one of the premier agents of the Shop, a secret U.S. contractor that handled international espionage affairs that the government wanted kept secret. The government also wanted plausible deniability. They were to handle things in their own way, and no one in the government needed to know what exactly that way was. If it all blew up, no one would know they even existed. Peter Smith was considered by many to be the Shop's finest agent. He didn't necessarily disagree although he attributed much of his success to remarkable luck, a notion he chose not to share with anyone else. On more than one occasion, he faced certain death, but he always managed to survive because of his training, his instincts and his remarkable luck. Fortunately, his friend and fellow agent Candace Kane was always around to witness his great escapes. He thought about what had transgressed at the Tenth Man. He may not have survived the night if she hadn't warned him that his life was in danger. It was remarkable luck.

Peter Smith loved Hawaii, and he had been looking forward to the mission there. The Shop had sent him all around the globe, chasing counterfeiters in the Caymans, assassins in the Seychelles, but there was just something special about Hawaii. Even tangling with The Pit wasn't so bad if he could just sink his toes in the warm sand. He had been on every island and knew them all well. He even joked that when he retired, he would become a tour guide there. But there was much to do before that time, and presently he needed to make his way to Maui and stop the Pit from their current scheme and keep from getting killed at the same time. This was a job for Xavier Carnahaha. He booked a later flight to Maui. The game was on.

Chapter 8

Feyodore Arbackle was not impressed by the man he was sitting next to on the plane. He had heard so much about the great Peter Smith that he expected more. The American agent must have had a good PR person because this man didn't seem formidable at all. He did play his undercover role well, though, because at times even Arbackle forgot he was an agent and not some random American on vacation with his wife. The presence of the woman also threw him off. While Peter Smith often worked with a woman, his intel said he would be traveling alone. This was why he planned to assassinate him on the plane. This was a complication he wasn't prepared for. He considered killing both of them, but he decided the woman would be a non-factor without Peter Smith, so he stuck to the original plan. Peter Smith would never set foot in Hawaii.

He waited a few hours into the flight before he decided to act. He didn't want to sit next to a dead guy any longer than he had to. He got up from his seat and slowly made his way down the aisle towards the bathroom. There were two people in line waiting to use the restroom, so the big man stood in line. A woman came out of the bathroom, and he shifted his stance. He tried turning sideways, but that didn't really create any more room. It became a dance between him and the other passenger as they leaned forward and backward and side-to-side to avoid coming in contact with each other or other passengers. The dance repeated itself when the second person left the restroom. "Whew","" Arbackle said to himself, "That is the most exercise I have gotten in days."

The restroom was empty, and before he went in, he wanted to warn those behind him that he might be a while, but he was afraid they might get the wrong idea. He squeezed into the small room. Extracting the vial of poison was not going to be easy. It was taped to his right leg just above the calf. He tried rolling up his pants, but he couldn't get them up far enough to reach the vial. Then he tried unbuttoning the pants and reaching down past the thigh to get the vial. That didn't work either.

Arbackle realized that the only way to reach the vial was by completely removing his pants, a task that would be a great challenge for the large man in the small space. But he had a mission. So, Arbackle leaned against the door and slowly began pealing his pants off. He put one foot on the toilet seat to gain some leverage. Then he slid the right side down to about the middle of his thigh. Then he shifted, putting his other foot on the toilet seat and eased the left side down. He repeated the process and finally got the pants to his knees. He pushed the pants down a little lower and reached the vial. He peeled it from his leg and gave out an involuntary "welp" as several leg hairs came with the tape.

He placed the vial of poison between his lips as he then struggled to pull his pants back up. He reversed the process he had just gone through. He hoped there wouldn't be any sudden turbulence that would disturb the vial between his lips. The last thing he wanted was to accidently kill himself on his first mission. It would also take the bathroom out of service for the rest of the flight. Fortunately, for everyone on the plane, Arbackle got his pants righted without incident and made it back to his seat.

The Russian had a plan. We would conceal the vial until the flight attendant served drinks, then he would sneak the colorless, odorless poison in his neighbor's drink. Peter Smith would drift off to sleep and never wake up.

It wasn't long before the flight attendant came and took the drink orders. The man he thought was Peter Smith asked for a Dr. Pepper. Arbackle requested one, too. Several minutes went by before she returned with the drinks. The man next to him was sleeping. The small sleep before the big sleep, Arbackle thought. His tray table was down, and Arbackle was eager to help the flight attendant with the drinks. He would even add a little extra to his neighbor's drink.

Arbackle took out the vial and was starting to remove the lid when the woman who said she was from Kentucky grabbed his arm.

"Did you say you were a preacher?"

"Yes, I did."

She slapped him on shoulder.

"Why, you're just the person we need. Can you bless these drinks?"

'The drinks?"

"Yes, the peanuts, too. You never know where the devil has been."

"Um…sure"

"That's great!"

The woman slapped his shoulder again, knocking the vial out of his hands and onto the floor. He put the drink down and started speaking.

"Lord..."

"Shouldn't we all bow our heads."

"Um...yeah. Please bow your heads."

Arbackle closed his eyes and bowed his head.

"Lord, please bless these drinks..."

"And the peanuts."

"Bless these drinks and the peanuts and all these fine people on this flight and may we all reach our destinations safely."

"Yes, all of us."

"Amen."

"Amen."

When he finished the prayer, he looked on the ground for the vial. It was gone.

Peter Smith was proving hard to kill.

Chapter 9

While Peter Smith did not make his scheduled flight to Hawaii, Candace Kane did. She had a seat in the row behind where Peter Smith would have been. She suspected the people who were after him would also be on the plane, so she watched and waited for them to reveal themselves. Someone she did not recognize was sitting in Peter Smith's seat. He was with a woman who appeared to be his wife. If the man hadn't been sitting in Peter Smith's seat, then he would not have looked suspicious at all.

The couple were soon joined by another man, a big man, a preacher who said he was from Missouri, but who seemed to have a hint of an eastern European accent. Candace wondered if the two men were working together, and she watched to see if anything was passed between them. She was shocked when she saw the big man return from the restroom with a vial of something that he was trying to hide. It was clear to her that they were definitely not working together. In fact, it appeared the big man might be trying to harm the other. She took quick action and knocked the vial out of his hand and stealthy retrieved it. Was it a coincidence that an attempt was made on the man sitting in Peter Smith's seat? She didn't know. But one thing was certain: the enemy had revealed himself, and he was king size.

Chapter 10

Duke knew that something wasn't quite right with the big man next to him. He wanted to share his suspicions with his wife, but she was too wrapped up in the book she was reading, and besides, he was practically sharing a seat with the big man, so there was no way of having a confidential conversation about him. Of course, he had no idea the big man thought he was someone else or that he had tried to kill him. All he knew is that for somebody from Missouri, he sure didn't know much about Missouri. Duke decided to play amateur detective and try to learn more about the man sitting next to him.

"So, have you ever been to Hawaii before?"

"Just once. I flew into Honolulu, but I never got out of the airport. I caught a connecting flight to Manilla."

"The Philippines? What were you doing there?"

"Our church is working with the government to help drug addicts there."

"Their president is Mucusus, right?"

"Right."

Arbackle found himself giving more information than he should have. That Peter Smith was a sly one. He had indeed traveled to Manilla, but it wasn't church business; it was for the Pit. He was trying to establish a base in Manilla for the Pit's heroin trade. The Mucusus government had taken a hardline stance on drugs, killing dealers and addicts all the same. That made recruitment particularly difficult. The Pit needed a connection in the Mucusus government, someone who could run interference for them. His sources told him the best man to approach was Criscoe Oila. He tried to make contact with him. He called his office and spoke to his assistant, but Oila wasn't available. He was preparing for a trip to Hawaii. He told his assistant that he would also be in Hawaii and would like to meet with him. He left his name and number. It would all come together after he was free of Peter Smith.

Arbackle had said enough. It was time for the American to tell his story.

"Is this your first trip to Hawaii?"

"Yes. We are going for our 25th anniversary."

"25 years? Congratulation to you both."

He raised his glass of Dr. Pepper to the couple.

"So, where are you staying?"

Because Duke didn't really trust the man next to him, he didn't want to be too specific.

"At a resort in Lahaina. What about you?"

"At a hotel."

It wasn't just any hotel. This one offered a jacuzzi suite for the same price as a regular suite. After this flight, nothing would be better than a little time in the jacuzzi.

"So, do you all have any plans while you are here?"

Daisy suddenly became interested in the conversation.

"We're doing a luau at our resort on Monday."

Daisy didn't mind sharing all their plans with the man that Duke didn't trust.

"Then a sunrise tour of the volcano on Wednesday. And we're taking the Road to Hana on

Friday."

Arbackle took note of Peter Smith's itinerary.

"That sounds like you have a good trip planned. I'm here on church business, but I'm sure we'll have some fun."

The fun, of course, would be killing Peter Smith and maybe even the woman posing as his wife.

The conversation ended there. Arbackle began plotting his next attempt at killing Peter Smith. Duke, on the other hand, was working on a theory about this man who was supposed to be from Missouri but who didn't seem to really know anything about Missouri. Could he be a 400-pound spy?

Chapter 11

When the plane landed on Maui, Arbackle immediately got up from his seat and started going through the overhead bin. He found his bag, grabbed it and went up to the front of the plane. The other passengers saw him coming and stayed out of his way, so they wouldn't get run over.

He was in a hurry to meet up with Dmitri Pontiacovich who would be assisting him on Maui. Dmitri was waiting outside of the security area.

"Hey Fatty, good to see you."

"Don't call me that. I'm undercover. Call me Samson."

"OK, SAAAMSON. But you look a lot like my friend Fatty."

"Listen, this is what I need you to do. There is a couple we are following, and..."

"What couple? I thought it was one guy?"

"Well, now it's a couple. The man is wearing a black and yellow hat, and it says, M-I-Z-Z-O-U."

"MIZZOU?"

"Yes, MIZZOU."

"What is MIZZOU?"

"It doesn't matter. Look for a guy with that hat and find out where they are going. Remember, just blend in. You're a guy looking for his luggage just like everyone else there. Don't do anything suspicious."

"Got it. I'm just looking for my luggage. Nope, that's not mine. Nope, that's not mine."

"What are you doing?"

"I'm rehearsing. I want to be an actor someday.

All good actors rehearse."

"Enough rehearsing. Go play your role."

Dmitri walked off repeating his line.

Chapter 12

Duke had never been happier to get off a plane. Not only was he about to spend a week in paradise, but he was also separated from the large man who had been practically sitting on him. He and Daisy waited their turn to start moving toward the front of the plane. As they entered the terminal, Duke was a little disappointed.

"Hmm, I guess we're not going to get leied."

"Excuse me."

"On TV whenever anybody lands in Hawaii, there's a beautiful young woman who welcomes them to Hawaii and puts a lei on them. But there's nobody here."

"That's just on TV."

"I was looking forward to getting leied."

"You keep talking like that and you'll never get laid."

Duke wasn't really listening to Daisy. He kept looking around for the welcoming committee.

Daisy grabbed him by the arm and pointed to a sign that said Baggage Claim. "This way," she said. Duke resigned himself to the fact that no one was going to give him a lei, and he and Daisy followed the signs to the baggage claim area.

There was a strange, little man at the baggage claim. He kept looking at all the luggage—every bag regardless of size, shape or color. Duke thought that was strange. Most people only look at luggage similar to their own. But this guy was looking at all the luggage. He would peak down at the name and then announce, "Nope, that's not mine." Every piece he looked at, "Nope, that's not mine." Then after a little while, he said, "I've seen that one before. That's still not mine."

He would periodically look around at other people waiting for their bags. At one point he seemed to look directly at Duke and mouthed MIZZOU. Then he continued to examine the luggage and talk to himself until Duke had picked up their bags and headed to the shuttle station. As they were leaving the baggage claim area, Duke heard him say, "The airline must have lost my luggage."

Chapter 13

Candace Kane ordered an Uber as soon as the plane landed. When the big man headed for the front of the plane, she quietly followed. No one noticed her. After years of working around men who demanded to be seen, she found it very easy to be a woman who didn't want to be seen at all. She followed the big man out of the plane. Upon leaving the secured area, he met up with a smaller man who seemed to be losing his hair prematurely. He was practically bald up front, but he borrowed some from the back of his head and combed it over the bald patch. Only the owner of the hair was fooled.

They stopped under a sign with two arrows. The first one was pointing to the right and read "Ground Transportation." The second one was pointing to the left read "Baggage Claim." After speaking for a few moments, the smaller man headed in the direction of the Baggage Claim. The bigger man remained under the signs. Candace followed the smaller man to see what he was up to. He went to the Baggage Claim area. There were three carousels, and moments after he arrived, a voice over a loudspeaker made an announcement.

"Passengers from Flight 352 from Phoenix, your baggage will be arriving on Carousel One."

The little man walked up to the carousel and began looking at all the baggage from that flight. Candace noticed that while he pretended to be looking for his luggage, he was really keeping an eye on the couple from Missouri. She was keeping an eye on him. Being a good spy, she looked around to make sure no one was keeping an eye on her.

Chapter 14

"He's taking the shuttle to a resort in Lahaina," Dmitri said when he returned. "We can follow."

The two Russians got into the little man's rental car and pulled into the loading zone behind some taxis. There were five of them between his car and the shuttle. Dmitri was focused on the shuttle when an airport officer came up to the car.

"This area is for cabs. You will need to move your car."

"I'm waiting for my cousin. He is a cripple. I must pick him up here."

"Listen, you can't park here."

"He is a cripple. He is in a wheelchair. I must wait here."

"You can't wait here."

The shuttle started to pull away, and Dmitri looked up at the cop.

"Fine, the cripple is your problem now."

He pulled out of the loading zone behind the shuttle van.

"So, what's the plan, Fatty? Do we follow them to the resort and then ZZZZZ."

He pulled his hand across his throat like he was slitting it.

"No ZZZZZ, yet. We're just going to see where they are staying. They'll be plenty of time for ZZZZZ."

They followed the shuttle to the Isle of Lahaina Resort.

"Hey, Fatty, this is a nice place. Do you want to stay here?"

"No, drive on. Come on drive before somebody sees us."

Chapter 15

Daisy and Duke boarded the shuttle. It would be an hour ride to the resort. Duke began to relax. The driver identified points of interest on the island as he drove. After fifteen minutes, they stopped at a traffic light. Duke looked all around, taking it all in. He looked at the car behind them and was stunned by what he saw.

"There he is!"

"There who is?"

"The guy from the plane. He's in the car behind us."

Daisy gave a peek behind, but she didn't see anything.

"Are you sure?"

"Yes, it's him. I'm telling you there is something funny about that guy."

"That's not him. Why would he be behind us? Do you think he's following us?"

"He might be."

"You're crazy."

"Listen, he's not from Missouri like he said he was. He's never even heard of Mizzou."

"So, what do you think?

"I don't know, maybe he's some kind of criminal. He's not a preacher, I can tell you that."

"Maybe he's just dumb. Did you ever think of that? There's a lot of dumb people in this world, and he might just be one of them."

"Or maybe he's a spy, a 400-pound spy."

"It doesn't matter because he's not following us."

Duke kept trying to look behind him, but he couldn't really see well from inside the van. Eventually, the shuttle pulled into the driveway of the resort, and the car behind it sped past. Maybe he was just imagining it all.

Chapter 16

Candace saw the couple from Missouri go to the shuttle stand and then watched the Russians pull into the loading area behind some taxis. The airport also had a spot for an Uber driver. Candace walked up to the car.

"Aloha, I am Duber, your Uber. Are you going to the Holiday Inn?"

"Listen, Duber, you see that guy in the car up there. That's my brother-in-law."

"Which one? The big one or the little one?"

"The big one."

"Why did your sister marry him?"

"It doesn't matter. I think he's cheating on her."

"Is he cheating on her with the little guy?"

"No, I don't think so. But I want you to follow them to see where they go. There's an extra twenty in it for you."

"OOOH, exciting!"

The woman in the Uber followed the men in the rental car who were following the couple in the shuttle. The shuttle pulled into the driveway of the Isle of Lahaina. The rental car drove on. The Uber followed the rental car to the Aloha Hotel.

"OOH, I think the big man is having an affair with the little man. Should I pull in?"

"No. Go across the street."

The car pulled into the Sunshine Inn across the street from the Aloha Hotel.

"This isn't the Holiday Inn."

"Um, Duber, I'm not really going to the Holiday

Inn. This place will be fine."

She gave him his tip.

"You know something. Your sister should get a divorce. He is a bad man. I can tell."

"Yeah, thanks. Listen, I'm going to need a ride this week. Can you help me out?"

"Certainly. Call me anytime."

"No, I don't think you understand. I want to buy your time for the next few days, starting now. How does $100 a day sound."

"Sounds good. Two hundred sounds better."

"Yes, it does. You have a deal."

"Oh, what fun, spending time with a beautiful woman, keeping watch on an ugly man and getting two hundred dollars a day. What fun!"

"I'm Candace, by the way. Candace Kane."

"Very good, Miss Kane."

"Call me Candy…Candace."

"OK, Candace. I'll stay here and watch across the street while you check in."

Chapter 17

Peter Smith traveling as Xavier Carnahaha boarded a
later flight for Maui. He appeared to be a very relaxed
tourist embarking on a trip to paradise. But he was
anything but relaxed. He subtly examined every
passenger near him. None looked familiar or
particularly dangerous. But someone was out to get
him, and those people rarely announce themselves.
He didn't seek out conversations, but sometimes they
came to him. After the pilot turned off the seatbelt
light, a flight attendant started moving up the plane.

"Can I get you something to drink?"

"I'm sure everything you have is wonderful. But I
brought my own."

He held up the bottle of water he purchased
before boarding the plane. He wasn't going to take
any chances. He didn't know who to trust. Someone
had betrayed him and his organization, and his life
was in danger. Beyond that, he was supposed to be
working a mission against the Pit. It was a shame.
Hawaii could be very relaxing when people aren't out
to kill you. Thanks to Candace, though, he had an
advantage over those who would do him harm. They
were hunting Peter Smith, but Xavier Carnahaha was
now hunting them.

"Well, aren't you a cutie!"

Peter Smith wasn't expecting that kind of reaction
from the flight attendant. He paused before
responding.

"Well, you're not so bad…"

Then he saw a little girl in the row in front of him

who had stood up in her seat. She had curly blond hair, and the flight attendant was right-- she was a cutie.

"Hi,"

"Well, hello."

She sized him up.

"What's your name?"

"Emily Marie McBain,"

"Well, hello, Emily Marie McBain? How old are you?"

She held up all the fingers on her right hand. Then with the help of her left hand, she lowered one and then another.

"Three. Are you three?"

She nodded her head.

"Well, good for you."

She continued to stare at him.

"You know what?

"What?"

"Momma says, 'Don't be afraid.' She says, "Everything is going to be all right."

"Well, your mother is right, Emily Marie McBain."

"Uh huh."

She sat down in her seat. Peter Smith smiled, and thanks to a cute, little, blond girl, for the first time in several hours, he began to relax.

The rest of the flight was fairly uneventful. No one even came close to killing him.

As he was exiting the plane, he looked at the little girl.

"Goodbye, Emily Marie McBain."

"Goodbye. Be good."

"I will," he said to himself. He exited the plane and rented a car and drove to the Paradise Motel. The name was misleading, but it was close to the Warrior's Den, the island's premier sports bar. If Candace was in Maui, she would find him there.

Chapter 18

Duber was anxious to get started.

"Where are we going tonight?"

"Is there a sports bar on the island?"

"A sports bar?"

"Yeah, a place where they have lots of TVs with football and baseball and they have sports decorations."

"And cheerleaders?"

"Yeah, I suppose they could have cheerleaders."

"You must mean the Warrior's Den."

"That sounds about right. Let's go there."

"Ooh, fun."

"But first I need you to run some errands."

"OK."

She handed him some cash.

"I need a University of Hawaii t-shirt. I want to blend in at the bar."

"You should dress like a cheerleader."

"Um, no. Here's a list of everything I need."

"OK."

Candace showered and got ready to go while Duber ran the errands. When he returned, he looked strangely at Candace who was staring into the mirror.

"What's the matter? You don't like red heads?"

He shook his head. She took off the wig and threw it on the bed. She put on another one.

"How about jet black?"

"No."

"Natural it is."

Duber handed her the bag. She took out the t-shirt and held it up to the mirror.

"Warrior Volleyball, huh?

"They're very popular."

"OK."

She looked at the collar for the size.

"Um, I thought I asked for a large."

"You'll look better in a medium."

She frowned.

"I don't really want to…Never mind. This will be fine."

She put the shirt on. It showed off her curves more than she liked which was not ideal for someone who didn't want to be noticed. But it would have to do. They left for the bar.

Ten minutes later they arrived at the Warrior's Den. As they walked in the door, they were greeted by a young woman in a green cheerleader's uniform.

"Welcome to the Den. Two?"

They both nodded their heads. She led them to a table. They sat down, and soon they were joined by another cheerleader.

"Hi, I'm Steph. Can I get you all something to drink?"

"Just water."

Duber frowned.

"Me, too."

Steph left the table, and Duber watched her walk away. Candace watched him watch her.

"Cheerleaders?"

"Yeah."

"I think I'll have a look around."

Candace got up from the table and started walking around the bar. The décor was dominated by the green and white of the University of Hawaii-- The Warriors. There were also some photos of surfers and canoers and more than a few with volleyball players. There were several TVs throughout the bar. Most were turned to ESPN which was showing highlights of the afternoon games. Others were showing a golf match.

The bar wasn't terribly crowded. Candace imagined it would be much busier later that night. On the south side of the bar, there was a sign that said "UHOOPS." Two basketball goals were set up there for customers to shoot baskets.

A man was at one of the goals. He tossed a ball, and it bounced off the rim. He tossed another that hit the backboard and bounced away. His third toss was an air ball. The man paused to sip his drink from a souvenir cup.

Candace approached the second hoop and picked up a ball. Without looking at the man next to her she spoke.

"Do you ever make it?"

She shot the ball, and it went in.

"Nope."

He shot again, and the ball went off the backboard.

"Didn't you ever play?"

"I never saw the purpose."

Candace shot again. The ball went through the net without touching the rim.

"Then why do you always go to these bars?"

"I like the drinks. This one is particularly good. It called the Green Machine. Besides no one ever bothers me at a sports bar, although there was this one time in a bar in Phoenix where a woman..."

"Saved your life."

"Yeah…Thanks for that. So, what's new at work?"

"That pig Winston Salem got my job."

"What does he call you- Sugar Kane?"

"Candy Kane."

"Oh, that's right. I'm sure he'll be perfect for that job. Anything else?"

"We have a traitor at the Shop."

"Do tell."

"We intercepted a phone call. It seems someone wants you dead."

"Me? Why?"

"I don't know. It's someone who pays in rubles."

"A Russian. Well, it must the Pit."

"I saw them—a big guy and a little guy."

"How big?"

"Huge. He was about 6'5", and he looked like he had eaten a whale."

"Fatty Arbackle."

"The other was smaller, dumber."

"Dmitri Pontiacovich."

"Do you know these guys?"

"Only by reputation."

"They tried to kill a guy from Missouri."

"Well, that's rude. What did Missouri do to deserve that?"

"I don't know, but I think they are going to try again."

"So, what's next?"

"We're going to a luau."

"Oh, I love a good party, especially a luau."

"It's tomorrow night at the Isle of Lahaina. If I'm

45

right, the Russians will be there."

"Splendid. It's a date."

"Not exactly. By now the traitor may be onto me. Besides, I already have a date."

She motioned towards Duber across the bar.

"Who's that?"

"That my Uber. His name is Duber."

"Duber the Uber, how nice. So, tell me, what does dear Duber know?"

"Nothing...yet."

"Ignorance is bliss."

"Yeah. Here."

She handed him one of the cell phones that Duber had picked up for her.

"I've already programmed my number in it. Where are you staying?"

"The Paradise Inn. What about you?"

"The Sunshine Inn."

"Are you and Duber sharing a room?"

"It's nice to meet you, Mr. Carnahaha. See you at the luau."

Chapter 19

Daisy and Duke were having a wonderful time in Hawaii. After checking into their room, they visited the open-air restaurant. All sorts of things were happening around them. It was mid-afternoon, and there were a few diners at tables having a late lunch, and several people were crowded around the bar. Small birds frequented the tables, reminding the diners that it was their territory. None of the diners seemed to mind the birds. After all, they were part of the atmosphere. Kids were playing in the pool adjacent to the restaurant while their mothers and other guests sunbathed. Beyond the pool was the beach and the Pacific Ocean. As they sat, members of a wedding party meandered through the restaurant on their way to an outdoor ceremony.

Daisy and Duke were sipping drinks, waiting for their food and taking it all in. Duke spoke.

"I can't believe we're really here."

"It's so beautiful."

They hadn't had a real meal in almost 24 hours, and that combined with the drinks and the atmosphere made Duke a little extra happy.

"Do you see that palm tree. It's in Hawaii. Do you know who else is in Hawaii? We are."

"Yes, we are."

"I'm going to take a picture of that palm tree."

He got up from the table, aimed his phone's camera towards the palm tree and took a photo of his forehead. He looked at the photo, saw that he hadn't operated the phone correctly and tried again. He then noticed a banana grove behind his chair.

"Hey look—bananas."

He took a couple photos of the bananas.

"Hey, take a picture of me with the bananas."

Daisy did as he requested, and as she finished, the food arrived. The couple ate their dinner and had another drink, and Duke took more photos of his forehead and of his surroundings. There were no spies in any of the photos.

They adjourned to their room where they sat on the balcony. They were on the tenth floor and were able to see the Pacific Ocean to their right, and the volcano to their left. "Do you see that. That's the Pacific Ocean. We are in the middle of the Pacific Ocean."

"Yes, we are."

"I've never been in the middle of the Pacific Ocean. Look over there. That's a volcano, a freaking volcano. Have you ever seen a freaking volcano?"

"No, never."

"Well, there's one right there. In a couple days we'll be at the top of that volcano."

"Yes, we will."

"Yes, we will, and do you know why?"

"Because you planned a wonderful vacation."

"Yes, of course, but do you know why we're going to the top of that volcano? Because we can."

"Yes, we can."

"Hey, do you feel that breeze? That's a Hawaiian breeze."

"Yes, it is. Uh, let's go in now."

The couple retreated to their room unaware of the dangers they would face in paradise.

49

Chapter 20

It was not paradise at the Aloha Hotel. While Arbackle had booked the jacuzzi room for the same price as a regular room, he had overlooked the fact that the room had only one bed. Dmitri wasn't happy.

"I can't sleep in this room."

"Why not?"

"There is only one bed."

"It's a queen bed."

"No."

"There will be plenty of room."

"No, I don't sleep in the same bed with another man. Besides, Fatty, you're too fat."

"I told you not to call me Fatty. Down here I'm Samson."

"OK, Samson, I am not going to sleep in the same bed as you. You are too fat."

"Look, it's a suite. You can sleep on the sofa."

"I don't want to sleep on a sofa. I want to sleep on a bed...by myself."

"I'll tell you what, we'll switch off. You can sleep on the sofa tonight, and I will sleep on it tomorrow night. OK?"

"OK for now."

Arbackle sat down in the jacuzzi.

"Are you coming in?"

"I don't want to get in a hot tub with another man."

"It's not a hot tub; it's a jacuzzi."

"I don't get in a jaaaa-cuuuuzi with another man. Besides you are too fat."

"Stop saying that. I'm big. I was born big."

"Yes, I've heard the story. You were 11 thousand pounds at birth."

"We have to talk about the plan. Are you getting in?"

"I can talk about the plan from here."

"I'm expecting a call from the mole any minute. I need to find out more information about Peter Smith. I'm just not sure that was him on the plane. He seemed too...soft."

"Soft Americans with their soft women and their soft...drinks."

"Besides he was traveling with a woman. He was supposed to be traveling alone."

Arbackle's phone rang, and he answered it.

"Hello...Yes, it's me...OK. Still no photo of him... Really? That's very interesting... Both of them...Right. No rubles. Listen, the ruble is a perfectly good form of currency...Right, no rubles. Got it."
Arbackle hung up the phone.

"Well, the mole says Peter Smith is in Hawaii, and he might be traveling with another agent, a woman. That must have been him on the plane. They said they were going to a luau tomorrow night, and that means we are going to a luau tomorrow night."
Dmitri took out his knife.

"And tomorrow night, it will be ZZZZZ for Peter Smith."

Chapter 21

Duke was looking forward to the luau. He bought a Hawaiian shirt just for the occasion. He called out to his wife who was still getting dressed in the bathroom.

"Hun, do you know what we are doing tonight?"

"We're going to a luau."

"Yes, we are, a real, genuine, Hawaiian luau."

"I'm very excited."

"It's all you can eat. Do you know how much I'm going to eat?"

"All that you can eat."

"That's right, and do you know what else, it's all you can drink, so you know what means?"

"You're going to drink more than you should."

"Yes, I am, and do you know why?"

"Because it's a genuine, Hawaiian luau."

"That's right. And do you know where we're going to sit?"

"Close to the stage, I hope."

"We'd better be close to the stage. I bought VIP tickets. It cost me an extra 30 bucks."

"I'm just glad it's at our resort, so we don't have to travel too far after you eat all you can eat and drink all you can drink."

"Yep. Are you about ready?"

"Yes, I am. How do I look?"

"Good enough to eat, but sorry lady, I'm going to a luau."

The couple took the elevator to the ground floor and walked to the luau entrance. They were met by two young Hawaiian women wearing grass skirts. The first woman took their tickets while the second one placed a flower lei on each of them.

"Look, Hun, we got leid in Hawaii."

"I'm very happy for you."

The woman who took their tickets told them they were at Table 4.

Chapter 22

Arbackle and Dmitri drove to a store to buy items for the luau. Arbackle found a Hawaiian shirt. It had images of the four islands in the midst of the Pacific Ocean, and across the front it read, "HAWAII"." Dmitri found a blue shirt with a large image of a brightly colored parrot.

"OK, let's go to the luau now," he said.

"One minute."

Arbackle stopped to look at some Panama hats. He tried one on and looked at himself in the mirror. Then he tried a couple more. The third one was the charm. The cashier rang up the merchandise, and he gave her a coupon for the hat and shirt combination. Then they paid for the merchandise and headed for the Isle of Lahaina.

The luau area was filling up as the men walked up. Arbackle approached the woman selling tickets and tried bluffing her.

"I had a buy-one-get-one-free coupon, but now I can't find it."

He feigned looking in his pockets.

"Can you give me a break here?"

"I'm sorry sir, everyone has to have a ticket to get into the luau."

"Listen, the show is about to start. Half the money is better than none."

"I'm sorry, you'll have to buy two tickets."

"Fine!"

He pulled some cash from his pocket.

"Do you want general seating or VIP?"

"Oh, you'd really like that wouldn't you? Charge me for two tickets and then try to get an extra $30. No, thank you. I'll be able to see everything I want from general admission."

Chapter 23

Candace emerged from the bathroom of the hotel wearing a bright yellow dress.

"You look very shiny in your yellow dress."

"Well, aren't you sweet. You don't look half bad in your Hawaiian shirt. Since you're Hawaiian, do you still call it a Hawaiian shirt? Or do you just call it a shirt?"

"What?"

"Oh, never mind."

The two left for the luau. Along the way, she asked him to stop at a store.

"Sure. What are you getting?"

"Oh, just girl stuff."

She went into the store and came out wearing a big hat and carrying a green shopping bag.

"Listen, Honey, we aren't just going to the luau for fun. Those men from the airport will be there."

"The big one-- your sister's husband-- and the little on?"

"I have a confession to make. He's not really my brother-in-law. I can't tell you anymore. But it might get a little hairy in there tonight. I don't want you to get involved, so if something happens, just let me handle it. OK?"

"This is all very exciting."

When they reached the luau area, Candace put the shopping bag in her large purse. She paid for the tickets, and one of the women approached to put a lei on her. She handed Duber her purse. He was surprised at the heaviness of the bag.

"What do you have in here?"

"Oh, just girl stuff."

"Girl stuff is very heavy."

Chapter 24

There were 100 tables set up in the luau area. It was mostly empty when Daisy and Duke arrived, but the two rows closest to the stage – the VIP area-- were filling up. Daisy and Duke found their table. Two other couples were already seated.

"You can start the party now. We're here."

Duke introduced himself to the table.

"I'm Duke, and this is Daisy."

One of the men at the table stood up. He pointed at Daisy.

"Daisy."

Then he pointed at Duke.

"Duke…Daisy-Duke…Look, honey, it's Daisy Duke. Is Uncle Jesse coming?"

The woman across the table from him stood up.

"I'm Rebecca. This is Milt."

Duke sat next to Milt. He was about the same age as Duke, and he was also wearing a Hawaiian shirt. Daisy sat across from Duke and next to Rebecca. Milt sold insurance in Boise, Idaho, and Rebecca answered phones at the local newspaper, the Statesmen. Milt started the conversation.

"Is this your first time in Hawaii?"

"It sure is, and this is our first luau."

"It's our first one, too."

A woman in a grass skirt brought a tray of drinks-- half were blue and the other half were orange.

"We have Blue Hawaii and Mai Tai."

The women took the blue drinks and the men had Mai Tais. Duke raised his glass.

"Cheers, Milt."

The two men drank and laughed and told stories about selling insurance in Idaho and working at a state university in Missouri. A casual observer might have thought they knew each other for years or that they were brothers because they looked and acted so much alike. After several minutes, a tall, well-tanned man in a Hawaiian shirt and white pants took the stage and announced that the pig was ready to be pulled from the sand. The crowd gathered around the pit, and two young men in grass skirts pulled the pig above ground and took it to the kitchen area. A few minutes later, the dinner began. The two couples got in the buffet line and filled their plates.

Chapter 25

Arbackle and Dmitri found a table close to the bar. They began to scan the crowd for Peter Smith. As the sun set, it became harder to see people's faces. Arbackle was about to give up on finding him when there was a flash of lightning and he saw him sitting at a table near the stage. He nudged Dmitri.

"There he is."

Dmitri responded, "When the time is right, I will..." He didn't finish his sentence but made a slashing motion.

"What?"

"I said when the time is right..."

"What?"

Dmitri gave up trying to talk with all the noise.

Chapter 26

Candace and Duber sat down at a table, and a waitress brought them some drinks. Candace started looking through the crowd. She saw the couple from Missouri first. They were close to the stage and would be fairly easy to watch. She was looking for the Russians when she received a text message. It was from Xavier Carnahaha.

"You look lovely in that dress, but the hat has to go."

"Where are you?"

"I'm watching our Russian friends. I spotted them when they came in."

"I've got the couple from Missouri."

"Good. Enjoy the show."

Chapter 27

The tall man returned to the stage and welcomed
everyone to the Isle of Lahaina Luau, "The best luau
on the island." He was very polished, and Duke
thought he was almost too polished. He would have fit
in at any lounge in the continental U.S. He said the
show would tell the story of the Pacific islands,
Hawaii, Tahiti and Samoa. He promised that the story
would be told with song and dance. Duke cheered.

"Yeah, that's what I came for, the hula girls."

Milt nodded and raised his glass in Duke's
direction. Three young women in short grass skirts
and bikini tops began dancing on the stage. The
announcer began telling the story of the islands. The
dancers didn't shake their hips or really even move
much. Mostly they danced with their hands. They
were followed by three young men who also danced
with their hands. Duke was not impressed.

"Hula boys? Who wants to see hula boys?"

Daisy responded.

"I do."

"Well, I want to see another Mai Tai. Do you want
one, Milt?"

"Sure, if you're buying."

"I'll be right back."

Duke made his way to the bar where he grabbed
two drinks. The sun had set, and there was scarce
light as he made his way back to the table. There was
a flash of light from above, and for a moment he could
see a little better. The light shined on a big man sitting
in the general admission area. He was sitting next to

a smaller man. Neither were watching the show on the stage. They seemed to be watching him. There was something familiar about the big man, but the quantity of rum he had consumed had slowed down his recall.

He got back to his table, handed Milt his drink, sat down and continued watching the show. The emcee was now telling the story of Tahiti. More women came out in short, grass skirts, but these dancers used their hips more than their hands. "That's what I'm talking about." Duke said. They were followed by more male dancers. When they took the stage, Duke turned away and there was another flash of light. He saw the big man again, and it all came back to him. That was the guy from the airplane. What was he doing here? He tried to get Daisy's attention, but the music was too loud, and she was more interested in the hula boys who were now shaking their hips. Duke looked back to where he saw the man. But it was dark, and he couldn't make out any faces. He felt something lightly touch his head. He looked around suspiciously, but he didn't see anything. Then he felt it again and again, and there was another flash of light. It was raining.

The emcee promised the show would go on despite the rain, and the staff started delivering clear plastic ponchos to the guests. Duke put his on, but Milt struggled, so Duke helped him.

"Thanks, buddy. I'm buying this round."

He got up and walked to the bar.

The emcee started talking about the Samoans, and Duke tried once again to talk across the table to Daisy.

"I saw him again."

"Who?"

"The big guy from the plane."

"I can't hear you."

She turned her attention back to the stage.

Milt returned with the drinks, and the Samoans started their fire dance. He approved.

"Whoo hoo! It's going to be a hot time in the ol' town tonight."

Chapter 28

The show concluded with all the dancers on the stage. The Russians began making their way to the VIP area. A couple people from the crowd got on the stage. Milt saw them and said, "Let's go buddy." He headed for the stage, and Duke followed. They made it onto the stage and started to do a cabaret dance, kicking their legs out. As they started dancing, Dmitri saw them.

"Look, it's the Rockettes."

Staff started removing the guests who had gone on stage. Just as they were getting to center stage, there was a bright flash followed immediately by a loud crash, and the skies opened up.

Arbackle tried to put on his poncho, but he had trouble finding the arm holes, and in the rain, it started clinging to him. The big Russian ended up with the poncho crumpled up around his shoulders as the rain came down. The smaller Russian never attempted to put his on.

The rain was too much for the audience, and many headed for shelter. Daisy and Rebecca hurried along with the crowd. Milt helped himself off the stage without the assistance of the security staff.

Duke was slower getting off the stage as he sat with his head down trying to catch his breath. In the chaos of the rain and the blur of alcohol, Milt sat down at the table where Duke had been sitting. When Duke finally made it back to the table, Milt was resting his head on it. "It's been fun," Duke shouted over the rain. Duke maneuvered through the crowd and joined his wife under the shelter.

With the rush of the crowd, the Russians had become separated. Arbackle was still struggling with his poncho, but Dmitri continued on his mission.

Candace got a text from Xavier. "The Russians split up. I'm on Fatty."
Dmitri had lost sight of his intended victim in the rush of the crowd. He looked to the stage, but he was no longer there. Then he saw Milt with his head on the table with his poncho on. He took out his knife.

Candace wasn't too far behind him. She was dodging people who were rushing for shelter. When the crowd cleared, she saw Milt sitting at the table, and like Dmitri, she mistook him for Duke. She feared she was too late. Then she saw Dmitri walking with a purpose. He was a couple steps ahead of her, and she struggled to reach him before he reached the man at the table. Just as Dmitri was about to strike, Candace struck him in the back of the head with her purse. The blow knocked him to the ground.

"I'm sorry, sugar. I just can't control this crazy, ol' purse. Are you alright?"
Duber had been following her, and he grabbed Dmitri's arm to both help him up and to make certain he didn't try to harm Candace.

Dmitri didn't say anything. He stared down at the ground looking for his knife which was lost amid the scrambling feet. Eventually, he gave up on finding it. He mumbled something and disappeared into the crowd. He met up with Arbackle who had found shelter under the bar. He had seen the scuffle and assumed Dmitri was being detained. He was relieved to have his partner back. They gave up on any more assassination attempts for the night and left the Isle of Lahaina.

Candace checked on the man at the table. To her surprise, he wasn't who she thought he was. She started to panic. She searched the crowd for Duke. Then she got a text message from Xavier.

"The Russians have left the building. I'm following Missouri to make sure he gets home safely. Good show."

Rebecca walked up to Candace.

"Sorry, honey, he's taken…although I wonder why sometimes."

Milt raised his head, cupped his chin in his hands and emitted a happy sigh. Duber came up to Candace carrying her purse. He reached in and took out a handful of D batteries.

"Your girl stuff is very interesting. Lots of interesting things at the luau."

He showed her Dmitri's knife which he had recovered.

"Lots of interesting things at the luau."

"Yeah, we need to talk."

Chapter 29

Candace told Duber all about The Shop and The Pit. He was fascinated.

"So, you are a spy."

"Yeah, something like that."

"And the big guy is a spy?"

"Yes."

"And the little guy?"

"It looks that way."

"Um…Am I a spy."

"Not officially."

"What about the man at the luau? Is he a spy?"

"No, he's just a tourist."

"And you saved him."

"Yes."

"Why?"

"Because it was the right thing to do."

"Then I want to be a spy. I want to be a spy like you."

Chapter 30

Candace's phone rang early the next morning. It was Peter Smith. Candace put him on speaker phone.

"How are you enjoying paradise?"

"I've left Paradise."

"You've what? How could you leave Hawaii at a time like this?"

"Easy, my dear. I haven't left the island. I've left the Paradise Motel."

"Where are you?"

"After I followed Missouri back to his room, I met up with my new best friend, Ella Mabella. She works as a concierge at the Isle of Lahaina, a lovely woman. She found me a room immediately above them."

"Well, that was convenient. And will Ella Mabella be joining you there?"

"Who says she's not here now? And what about Duber the Uber? I assume he's there with you. Did you all have yourselves a night?

"Duber is here, and that's all you need to know. I've told him everything."

"Very good. Welcome to the team."

"It's been very fun. Very exciting."

"I'm sure it has been. So, we need to find out what are Russian friends are up to. Candace, why don't you sashay on over there and see what you can find out.

"First, I can walk. I can creep. I can stroll. I can even saunter. But I do not sashay. Also, I think the big guy has already made me. I should keep my distance."

"Well, that's unfortunate. I suppose it's up to me."

"I'm not sure that's such a good idea. These guys are here to kill you. We can't just send you in there. That would be insane."

"Do you have any other ideas?"

Duber spoke up.

"I'll go."

Candace was concerned.

"I'm not sure about this."

"It's OK. I'm a native. They won't even notice me."

"This might work."

"I don't know."

"I want to help."

Peter Smith gave Duber his instructions.

"OK, Duber, this is what you need to do. When you go over there, find a maid, and tell her you need some towels. Then head over to the Russians' room with the towels. Offer to take them to the bathroom. Then look around for anything useful."

"Got it."

Chapter 31

"So, Fatty, who is this big shot you are meeting with?"

"His name is Criscoe Oila. He is the Minister of Executions or something like that. If we can make this deal, I'll be on my way up. No one will be calling me Fatty anymore."

There was a knock on the door. Dmitri answered it. Duber was there holding some towels.

"What do you want?"

"Did you ask for some towels?"

"Oh great, more towels."

"We wouldn't need so many if you hadn't used them all with the jacuzzi."

"Hey, I'm a big guy. I need lots of towels."

"Should I put them in the bathroom?"

Arbackle's phone rang, and he turned all his attention to it. Duber took the towels to the bathroom. He looked around for anything useful.

"Hello, Mr. Oila. This is Feyodor Arbackle...No, that's my father. I'm Feyodor Jr....Yes, Fatty....Yes, a lot of people think it's funny. Listen, Criscoe, can I call you Criscoe? Good. I understand you are on Maui. Your people say we might be able to meet...Lunch today...at the Green Gill...1:00. I'll see you there."

Duber left the room as the phone call ended. He returned to the hotel across the street. Candace was on the phone with Peter Smith.

"He's back."

She placed her phone on speaker and put it on the table. Peter Smith questioned him.

"So, what did you see?"

"Nothing much. They are really sloppy. There was a lot of trash and towels. They were everywhere."

"Great, so they are sloppy and wet. That's not much to go on."

Candace jumped in.

"Did you see anything else?"

"No."

Peter Smith was disappointed.

"Well, we will have to figure out something else."

"I can tell you where he is eating lunch."

"Oh."

"Yeah, he got a phone call while I was there. The man's name was Oila. He called him Criscoe.

"Did you say 'Criscoe Oila'?"

"Yes."

"You're sure it was Criscoe Oila and not Canola Oila or Olive Oila?"

"It was Criscoe. They are having lunch at the Green Gill."

Candace was encouraged.

"Is that helpful?"

"It's interesting."

"Why? Who is Criscoe Oila?"

"He's a Philippian official."

"Why is he meeting with the Russians?"

"That's something I will find out at lunch."

"Peter, are you sure that is wise?"

"Trust me, my dear. They won't even know that I am there. You did great, kid. You might be pretty good at this spy business, after all."

"Thanks."

"Well, you all have fun. Don't do anything I

wouldn't do."

Chapter 32

Daisy was sitting on the balcony reading and enjoying the beautiful day when Duke stumbled out.

"Morning, Glory."

"Hmmm, yeah."

"Did you have a little too much to drink last night."

"Maybe."

"Do you remember getting on the stage?"

Duke paused before he answered, and then he smiled.

"Yep."

"Well, I'm glad you had a good time."

"Let's do it again tonight."

"I think we are just going to take it easy today. We have an early morning start tomorrow."

Duke looked at the volcano.

"Sunrise at Haleakala. That will be something to see."

"What time does the shuttle pick us up?"

"2:00."

"That's early."

"It takes a while to drive up to the top."

"Yeah, well, why don't we go down and get some breakfast."

The couple went to the open-air restaurant to eat. A wedding party walked by.

"Another wedding. Do you think I should give then some advice and let them know what it takes to stay married 25 years?"

"And what is that?"

"Alligator love."

"And crocodile kisses?"

"You bet."

"I think they need to learn that on their own."

"So, what's on the agenda for today."

"I think I will just sit by the pool and enjoy the day."

Duke saw a beautiful woman in a bikini walk by.

"Yeah, me too."

The couple finished their breakfast and went to the pool. Duke picked up a copy of the Honolulu Star Advertiser and began scanning the headlines.

"Is there anything interesting in the news?"

"Not really."

"No robberies or murders or spies?"

Duke lowered the paper and looked over to her.

"You know, I saw him last night."

"Who?"

"The big guy from the plane. I'm telling you, there is something funny about him."

"That's right, he's a 400-pound spy."

"He could be. This whole place could be swarming with spies."

"Sure. They all want to know all your secrets."

"I'm going to keep an eye out for him."

"You do that. I'm going to read."

Chapter 33

Peter Smith arrived at the Green Gill a few minutes
before one. He was wearing sunglasses and a
Panama hat and holding a copy of the Honolulu Star
Advertiser. The Green Gill was a casual seafood
restaurant. Painted on the door was a giant smiling
fish who had a fishing line coming out of his mouth
which was connected to a fishing pole.

"Welcome to the Green Gill. Just one today?"

Peter Smith was greeted by a young man wearing
a yellow Green Gill t-shirt with the same fish on it. His
name tag said PICKLE.

"Well, hello, Pickle."

"It's pronounced PI-kel."

"I'm sorry."

"That's OK, nobody gets it right. My manager still
calls me Pickle."

"Maybe you should change it."

"Maybe I should. But, you know, it's been my
name for 19 years."

"I understand. Well, PI-kel, I am meeting
someone who is running late. Do you mind if I just sit
and wait?"

"Oh, sure."

Peter Smith sat down on a bench and opened up
the newspaper. It shielded him from others in the
restaurant. After a few minutes, a man burst through
the door. Peter Smith knew by the sound it had to be
the large Russian. He kept his nose on the news.

"Welcome to the Green Gill. Just one today?"

"No, I'm meeting someone."

"Would you like me to seat you now or would you like to wait?"

"I'll wait."

He sat down next to Peter Smith who shifted to make room for the Russian and to keep himself covered by the newspaper. It wasn't long before Criscoe Oila arrived.

"Is that you, Fatty? It's got to be you?"

"It's me. But you can call me Samson."

Oila laughed.

"I like Fatty."

"OK. Let's get a table. Hey, Pickle, give us a table where we can talk some business."

"It's PI-kel."

"Huh?"

"My name, it's pronounced Pi-kel, not pickle. Everybody gets it wrong."

"Whatever. Just give us a table where we can have some privacy."

"OK."

Peter Smith peaked around the newspaper to see where the Russian and the Philippian were seated. When Pickle returned, he got up.

"Well, Pi-kel, my date is running later than I thought. I think I will have a seat."

He crept closer to the host so he could whisper in his ear.

"And it's a private lunch, if you know what I mean. So, could you put us somewhere discreet, and he motioned his head in the direction of the other men."

"Oh, I understand. Someone is having lunch with someone he shouldn't be having lunch with."

"Something like that."

Pickle led him to the same section of the restaurant where the other two men were seated. There were no other diners in the section. Pickle gave him a menu.

"Can I get you something to drink?"

"Yes, an iced tea, please."

"Would you like it in a signature cup?"

"I would... And PI-ckle. When my date comes in, please show her to my table. She has long, red hair and a lovely smile."

"Ooh, a red headed stranger. Wicked."

Pickle left, and Peter Smith discreetly pulled out a thin receiver about the size of a calculator. The writing on it read "Nosey Neighbor." He had picked it up at Walgreens in their "As Seen On TV" section. Then he inserted a small headphone in his ear. He adjusted the receiver, aiming it towards the table with the two men. He heard the Philippian laughing.

"I like you, Fatty. You're a good sport. So, what can I do for you and the Pit?"

"So, Criscoe, you are the Minister of Executions or Punishment?"

The Philippian laughed heartily.

"The minister of Discipline."

"So, you are in charge of executions?'

"You could say that."

"Many people are being executed these days."

"Only those who deserve it-- those killers and the ones in the drug trade. They are enemies of the state."

"Oh sure, but it does seem like a waste. What if some of those enemies of the state became friends of ours."

"Impossible. All enemies of the state must be executed."

"What if some of the men who are "executed" aren't really executed?"

"I'm not sure I follow."

"You are executing so many men these days that no one is going to miss a few dozen who might slip through the cracks."

"That would be treason."

"One man's treason is another man's treasure."

Oila paused for a few seconds.

"Tell me more."

Arbackle explained the plan. The Pit was trying to set up a drug pipeline from China through the Philippines to Hawaii and eventually to the mainland United States. They needed some people in the Philippines, and they couldn't exactly fill these positions with a job fair. The best candidates would be those with experience and who knew the territory. Convicted drug dealers would be perfect especially since officially they would already be dead. They had nothing to lose, and they were expendable. Criscoe Oila would choose the men...for a piece of the action, of course.

Oila laughed loudly.

"I like you, Fatty. This is a good plan. I think you and I are going to work together well. Of course, I am going to need a little start up financing."

"How much?"

"$500,000."

"That's a lot of money."

"There's a lot to be done—finding the men, getting them new identities, etc."

"Do you think you can do it for a little less?"

Criscoe Oila laughed.

"No."

The two men agreed to start working together as soon as Arbackle delivered the start up financing. Peter Smith removed the earpiece and slid it and the received into his pocket. Pickle came moments later.

"Well, here she is."

A confused young woman with red hair was accompanying him.

"There you are," Peter Smith said. "Sit down…Pickle, get her something to drink."

After Pickle left, the woman spoke.

"Um, do I know you. I was supposed to meet my friend here, but she cancelled. But the host said you were waiting for me."

"Well, Pickle is a bit confused. But let's not disappoint him. It seems we are both here alone. We night as well be alone together."

"Well, OK."

"I'm Xavier, Xavier Carnahaha."

Chapter 34

After the meeting with Oila, Arbackle had to report back to Moscow.

"Oila is in. He will supply the labor in the Philippines, but he wants some start up cash…$500,000…I know that's a lot of money…No, he won't take half in coupons…Well, I don't know. Don't we have some kind of budget for bribing government officials…Oh, well, when does the next fiscal year begin… I don't think we can wait that long...Thank you. I appreciate you looking into it...No, he's still alive…Listen, he's their top agent. Killing him has proved harder than we thought…Don't worry, we have a plan…Tomorrow, at the volcano…No, we are not going to throw him in the lava. Who throws people in lava? Besides, it's not that kind of volcano…Dormant… It's inactive…He's taking a sunrise tour. We'll get him then…I understand. No money for Oila while Peter Smith is still alive."

Chapter 35

After lunch, Peter Smith called Candace who was curious about what he learned.

"So, how was lunch?"

"Very informative. The Russians are trying to use the Philippines as part of an international drug operation, and they need some local talent, if you know what I mean. Apparently, they imagine a "Manilla to Honolulu connection.""

"So, that explains why they are here in Hawaii."

"True. But it doesn't explain why they are trying to kill Mr. and Mrs. Missouri."

"How are the lovely couple?"

"Still alive. They are staying close to home today, but tomorrow they are headed to the volcano to watch the sunrise."

"That's probably when the Russians will make their next move."

"Agreed. So, this is the plan. You and Duber head up in his Uber. I'll ride on the shuttle with the tourists and try to find out what they have done to earn the ire of the Russians."

"The sun rises at 6:07."

"Good. Let's make certain our little couple also sees the sun set."

Chapter 36

Thanks to his Nosey Neighbor, Peter Smith was able to learn which shuttle Daisy and Duke were taking, and he made reservations for the same tour. The shuttle would be picking up passengers from several resorts in the area, and the Isle of Lahaina would be one of the first stops. Peter Smith met up with the couple at the shuttle stop at 1:45.

"So, I guess this is the place."

Daisy spoke to Peter Smith.

"Are you taking the tour of the volcano, too?"

"I am."

"I'm Daisy, and this is Duke."

"I'm Xavier."

Daisy was skeptical.

"Really? I am sorry for saying this, but you don't really seem like an Xavier."

"Well, that is very clever of you. You are correct. My name is not really Xavier. I'm going to let you all in on a little secret. I am a spy."

Duke was astonished.

"What?"

"Yes, I'm working undercover for the state's Department of Tourism to evaluate the tour guides."

"So, they set you up with a fake name and everything."

"Yes, but it's not as exciting as you might think. This is the ninth time I have taken this tour this year."

"So, that's all you do is ride around on different tours?"

"Yes. There is much to see in Hawaii, and we

want to make sure the tourists have the best experiences."

"Wow. Who knew?"

"Practically no one, so I would appreciate it if you kept my little secret to yourselves."

"Sure thing, Xavier."

Duke winked at him.

"So, where are you all from?"

Daisy spoke up.

"We're from Columbia, Missouri. We both work at the University of Missouri."

"Oh, so am I traveling with Professors Duke and Daisy? I better check my grammar."

"No, I'm the administrative assistant to the associate dean for Computer Aided Design, Graphics, Artificial Intelligence and Related Special Projects."

"Wow, that's a mouthful. It must take you twenty minutes just to answer the phone."

"I just say 'Dr. Incantango's Office.'"

"And you, Duke, tell me all your secrets."

"Well, I'm a spy, too."

"Are you?"

"Not really. I just wanted to see what it was like to say it. Duckworth, Duke Duckworth."

"Very nice."

"I work in procurement. I am a buyer for the University's Hospital."

"So, you purchase equipment like respirators."

"I purchase everything—respirators, thermometers, even bedpans."

"What about pharmaceuticals?"

"Normally not. We usually have a separate buyer for them, but our last one recently had a terrible accident, so I had to pick up some of his work."

"Interesting. Is this your first time in Hawaii?" Daisy joined in.

"It's our first time being anywhere," Daisy said.

"So, you've never been out of the country—to Europe or Africa or Russia?"

"No."

"Interesting. Well here comes our van. Remember, mums the word."

Chapter 37

Dmitri had questions about the next mission.

"I don't understand. Why does it take four hours to get to the top of the mountain?"

The men got in the car.

"It's not a mountain. It's a volcano."

"It looks like mountain to me."

"Well, it's a volcano."

"So, why does it take so long to drive up the volcano?"

"Because you have to have to drive around it until you get to the top."

"They should build a road that goes straight up. It would take fifteen minutes, tops"

"You can't drive straight up a mountain."

"It's a volcano."

"Anyway, we have to be there before the sun rises. That's when Peter Smith will be there."

"So, what is the big deal about a sunrise from the top of a volcano. Is it the same sun from the bottom of the volcano?"

"Well, yes, but it's something you don't see every day."

"I see the sun every day."

"Not from the top of a volcano."

"Except when it's cloudy. Then I don't see the sun."

"It's something people do."

"So, what do we do when we get to the top?"

"We look for Peter Smith."

"Then what?"

"While everyone's attention will be on the sunrise. Ours will be on Peter Smith."

"And then we ZZZZZ."

"Yes, then we ZZZZZ."

Chapter 38

After picking up the passengers from all the resorts, the shuttle began its accent of Haleakalā. The driver began his presentation.

"Thank you for joining Maui Waui Island Tours as we begin our accent of Haleakalā which literally means 'the house of the sun.' The volcano is the most dominant feature on the island of Maui and it takes up 75 percent. At its highest peak, Haleakalā is 10,023 feet above sea level. It will take approximately three and half hours to reach our destination this morning. Sunrise is at 6:07, so we should be there in plenty of time. I hope you used the restroom before we left because we won't be making any pitstops, and I hope you dressed warmly because you will find it significantly cooler at the top. Feel free to look out the window as we drive, but you aren't likely to see much as it is dark."

The passengers laughed at the last remark, and Duke looked over to Peter Smith and gave a thumbs up. Peter Smith nodded in his direction. The shuttle continued its long crawl up the volcano. As it neared the peak, the driver began his announcements.

"We are nearing our destination. I want to remind you that you are traveling with Maui Waui Tours, and we are shuttle number nine. There will be several tours here this morning, so make certain as you depart you get on the right shuttle. There are restroom facilities at the peak."

"Oh, thank God."

A woman in the back was relieved. The other passengers laughed and nodded to one another and affirmed they too were glad there were facilities available. The shuttle pulled to a stop.

"It is currently 5:55, and the sun will rise in about twelve minutes. Find yourself a good spot to observe but be careful around the edge. It's a long, bumpy fall into the crater.

"Natives have been living on Haleakalā for over one thousand years, and while it has become part of the national park system, natives continue to live on the volcano. Haleakalā is a sacred place, and if we are lucky today, we may be joined by some natives who will chant while rejoicing the rising of the sun. Enjoy the moment."

The tourists unloaded from the van and began making their way to the restrooms. Daisy and Duke started following them, but Duke stopped and zipped up his jacket.

"I'm glad you brought these coats. It's cold up here."

"Sometimes your wife knows what she's doing."

"I'm going to skip the restroom and go stake out a place for us."

"If that's what you want, but I have to go."

"You go. I'll be along the edge. But don't take too long. Some Hawaiian woman might come lay a claim on me."

"Dream on."

Duke walked towards the edge. A few people were gathering, and Duke found a spot, looked out along the horizon and then walked on. He found a second spot but then settled on a third. He was very excited about the upcoming sunrise, and he had a hard time standing still. While he waited for his wife, Duke became curious about the view at the bottom. From the spot he had chosen, he could see the outer edge of the volcano, but he couldn't quite see into the crater. The rocky ledge in front of him came up to his shoulders. So, he put his hands down on it and raised himself up with his arms to try to get a peek at the bottom. He had no idea that someone else was watching him and looking for just this sort of opportunity.

Chapter 39

Peter Smith tried calling Candace as the shuttle prepared to stop, but he had no cell service. He wondered if they had made it to the peak. He got up to exit the shuttle along with the tourists. An older couple was between him and the Duckworths. They took a few steps towards the front, and then the man fell down.

"Oh, for heaven's sake. What are you doing?"

"It happened again."

Peter Smith helped the man get back on his feet while still trying to keep an eye on Daisy and Duke. The man rested his arm on one of the seats and picked his leg up and started bending it and rolling it around.

"Cartilage."

"Excuse me."

"Cartilage. I have cartilage rolling around my knee, and sometimes it wedges itself in just the right spot, and boom, knocks me flat on my tookus."

"You should have that looked at."

"I'm having surgery when we get back to Ohio. I didn't want to do it before the trip."

The man seemed to regain his ability to walk and took a few steps to the front. Then he carefully exited the shuttle. Peter Smith followed and immediately started looking around for Daisy and Duke. He couldn't see them. He hurried down to the restroom. The facility had four urinals and four stalls. He glanced at the men standing, but none of them was Duke. Two of the stalls were occupied, and he decided to wait to see who came out. He washed his hands and kept an eye on the two stalls. No one came out. Then he started drying his hands slowly. Still no exit. At last, one of the stalls opened, and a man he didn't recognize came out and started washing his hands. Peter Smith was anxiously looking at the last stall, and the door started to slowly open. A small boy emerged. The man who had been in the other stall called out to him. "Hermie, come on over and wash your hands." Peter Smith quickly exited the facility and started looking around in all directions. Duke was nowhere to be seen. What had he done?

Chapter 40

Candace and Duber were a few minutes behind the shuttle carrying Peter Smith and the tourists. They were nearing the peak when traffic came to a complete stop. Duber got out to see what the problem was. He returned after a minute.

"What's going on?"

"Goat."

"What?"

"A goat is blocking the road."

"A goat?"

"Yeah, and he's a real mean one."

"Can't they just move him?"

"Nope. He charges anybody who gets close."

"Yeah, but he's just a goat."

"But he doesn't know he's just a goat."

"So, we are just supposed to sit here because of an angry goat who doesn't know he's a goat?"

"He lives on the volcano. We are just guests."

"Oh brother."

Chapter 41

Arbackle and Dmitri had arrived at the peak at nearly the same time as the Maui Waui shuttle. As they got out of the car, Dmitri began rubbing his arms.

"It's too cold."

"Yeah, who knew it would be this cold in Hawaii."

Dmitri rubbed his arms faster.

"It's too cold. I'll wait in the car."

"You can't wait in the car. We have to kill Peter Smith."

"You kill him. I'll wait in the car."

"Oh, it's not that bad. It's like going swimming. It's cold at the start but it gets better. After a few minutes, you won't even know that it's cold."

"I don't swim."

Dmitri got in the car and started it.

"Ugh! If you want something done right, you have to do it yourself."

Arbackle started observing people as they gathered around the peak. There wasn't much light, so mostly he saw shadows. The Maui Waui shuttle stopped near him, and tourists began to get off. The van's lights remained on as the tourists got off, and Duke appeared in the light.

"That's him."

Arbuckle whispered to himself.

"That's him. It's really him."

He started following the man he thought was Peter Smith. The man stopped a couple times before coming to rest at a spot on the edge of the volcano. The big man headed in that direction. He got closer and closer. Then the man he was watching raised himself off the ground. The perfect opportunity had presented itself. He started to walk faster. He was just a few feet away when he heard a voice,

"I see what you are doing, and you had better knock it off."

Arbackle stopped in his tracks and looked around to see who was speaking. Daisy rushed past him and went up to Duke.

"What do you think you are doing?"

"I wanted to see the crater," Duke said, and he lowered himself down.

"What if you fell? I hate to tell you, but your life insurance policy isn't that great."

"I wasn't going to fall."

Arbackle whispered to himself.

"Oh yes, you were."

Chapter 42

Daisy and Duke were oblivious to the danger around them. They were focused on the imminent sunrise. It was now crowded along the edge of the volcano. Everyone's eyes were focused on the horizon. Well, almost everyone. Feyodor Arbackle inched closer and closer to the man from Missouri. As soon as the sun rose over the peak, the man he thought was Peter Smith would go over the edge. It would be a terrible accident.

Duke took out his phone and aimed it at the horizon. Arbackle was right behind him. Duke held the phone slightly above his head to snap a few "before" photos, and then decided to switch to video, but he touched the wrong button, and instead of taking video, he turned the focus of the camera to the front of the phone. He then tried to take corrective action but instead clicked on the flash. Arbackle was looking directly at the phone when the light from the flash came on, and the light temporarily blinded him. Duke kept trying to make the camera do what he wanted, but nothing he did turned off the flash from the phone which kept sending the light into the Russian's eyes. Arbackle turned away from the phone and took a couple steps back while he tried to regain his vision. Duke brought the phone down and finally was able to reset the camera and start the video just before the first glimpse of sunlight came over the edge. The Russian blinked several times, but all he could see was a prism of colors. Once he regained his sight, he realized someone else had moved directly behind his intended victim.

The sun broke through the volcano's edge lighting up the sky and creating one of the greatest sights Daisy and Duke had ever seen. A native began to chant.

"Ka-lā.

'O ka lā ia.

Hau'oli mākou i kahi lā hou.

Mahalo, e ke Akua, no kahi lā hou.

Ua lawe 'oe iā mākou mai ka pouli a i ka mālamalama.

'Oli'oli.

'O ka lā ia.

He lā hou kēia."

Daisy was enjoying the experience.
"This is great. I wonder what it means."
Peter Smith who had maneuvered behind them spoke:
"The sun.
It is the sun.
We rejoice a new day.
Thank you, God, for a new day.
You have taken us out of the dark and into the light.
Rejoice.
It is the sun.
It is a new day."

Chapter 43

The crowd continued to enjoy the spectacular site for a few minutes and then began to break up. Daisy turned to Duke.

"That was a wonderful experience."

"Yes, it was. Now I have to use the bathroom."

"You're so romantic."

"Huh…Hey, I really enjoyed it, but now I need to go."

"Go. I'll meet you on the van.'

"OK." He then paused. "Hey, Hun, alligator love."

"And crocodile kisses."

She shook her head as she walked to the van as Duke headed towards the restrooms.

Chapter 44

Dmitri was in the car listening to the only radio station he could tune in at the top of the volcano. It was a classic country station. Dolly's Parton's Jolene was playing, and he became emotional.

"Jolene is going to steal that woman's husband. Jolene is no good."

As he wiped a tear from his face, he saw the man who was supposed to be dead walking toward the restroom.

"Uh oh! Time to go to work."

He got out of the car and started walking towards the restroom. He mumbled to himself along the way.

"Jolene is no good."

He was carrying a new knife since he had lost his other one at the luau. He held the knife in his hand and put it against his body, so no one could see it.

Chapter 45

Duke's entrance to the restroom was blocked by a little boy. He looked to be about three or four and he had a half-eaten banana in his hand. He was wearing a red and yellow Iron Man coat.

"Well, hello. Are you Iron Man?"

The little boy shook his head and offered up his banana to Duke.

"No thanks, little fella, I'm stuffed."

He inflated his cheeks. The little boy reached into his mouth and pulled out a piece of banana and offered it to Duke. Duke laughed and shook his head.

"No, thanks."

Just then the boy's father appeared.

"There you are."

He swept him up in his arms. The boy dropped the banana, and pieces of it fell on the sidewalk.

"Bye, Iron Man," Duke said, and he entered the restroom. He was the only one inside, and he started singing quietly as he took care of his business.

"Alligator love, and crocodile kisses. Havin' us a time, just me and my missus…"

Chapter 46

As Dmitri neared the restroom, he shed another tear, feeling the anguish of the woman singing the song.

"Jolene is bad."

The tear partially obstructed his vision, and he didn't see the discarded banana pieces on the ground. He stepped on a piece with the front of his foot, slipped forwards and hit his head on the door frame and then fell backwards. The blow didn't knock him out, but it did make him see stars and lose his orientation for a few seconds. He got to his feet but stayed bent over, collecting himself.

He didn't notice Duke who walked right past him. Duke didn't notice him either as he hummed his song. After a few seconds, Dmitri righted himself and walked into the restroom, but there was no one in the facility. He shrugged and looked at himself in the mirror. A red and purple whelp was already forming on his forehead. He brought his fingers to his head and touched it, but then jerked them back in reaction to the pain. He walked back to the car and didn't even notice he had dropped his knife in the grass.

Chapter 47

The goat which had stopped traffic near the top of the volcano eventually got tired of all the attention and trotted off the road and out of sight. Traffic began moving immediately, and Duber and Candace were able to reach the peak of the volcano a few minutes after sunrise. Duber pulled the car to a stop.

"You start over there by the restroom, and I'll walk the edge of the volcano," Candace said.

Duber nodded and headed towards the restroom. He looked inside the facility but didn't see anyone he recognized. As he was leaving, he noticed something shiny in the grass. He picked up a knife and looked around in all directions. No one seemed to be looking for it, so he stuck it in his pocket and continued looking around.

Chapter 48

Candace spotted the big Russian right away. He walked towards a car and got in. She heard Peter Smith's voice from behind her.

"You missed a great sunrise."

"Goat."

"Excuse me."

"Never mind. So, is everything OK up here?"

"Spectacular."

"Where's the couple from Missouri?"

"They're back in the shuttle, safe and sound. And you saw the Russians?"

"The big one, yes. Hard to miss him. So, you saved the day?"

"Something like that."

"So, what's next?"

"Well, I've got to get back on the shuttle before it leaves. We'll visit more after we get to the bottom."

"OK."

She never looked in his direction. She assumed he walked on. A few seconds later, Duber found her.

"Did you see anything interesting?"

"Lots of interesting things at the volcano."

He took the knife out and showed her.

"Lots of interesting things."

Chapter 49

Arbackle opened the passenger side door to the car and got in. Dmitri greeted him.

"You failed again."

"You know, I could have used your help out there…Wow, what happened to you?"

He pointed to the whelp on Dmitri's head.

"Sneak attack."

"What?"

"I followed the American after you failed, and then sneak attack."

"Really!?"

"I need another knife."

"He got your knife?"

"Grrr. What happened to you?"

"He temporarily blinded me."

"The American looks weak and stupid, but he is not."

"No, he is not."

They drove down the volcano mostly in silence.

Chapter 50

Peter Smith was one of the last passengers to return to the shuttle. He winked at Daisy and Duke as he went by. The bus driver spoke.

"Did you all enjoy the sunrise?"

The tourists universally agreed that it was a great experience.

"Don't forget, we have a sunset tour as well. If you would like more information about that or any of our other tours, you can go to our website at Mau Waui Tours Dot Com. It looks like we are ready to depart. Take a look and make sure you have everything you came with, and we will be on our way."

The bus began the trip down the volcano. Daisy unzipped her coat.

"What time will we get back to the resort?"

"About 11:00."

"Did you get some good pictures?"

"I don't know. I had a little trouble with the camera. I think I have a video of the sunrise."

The two looked at his photos on his phone. There were a couple of his forehead with just a hint of light. One was of the ground. There were a few pre-sunrise photos. The couple mostly focused on the video which caught the sun peeking out with the sound of the chanting in the background. They both agreed it was a great video and one they would watch often.

There was one photo that the couple paid little attention to because it was out of focus, and it was clearly a mistake. At first, it looked like just another photo of his forehead, but if they looked very closely,

they could have seen in the blackness a blurry,
startled expression of a Russian agent.

Chapter 51

As they took off down the volcano, Daisy was reading one of her books on her tablet, and Duke put his head back on the seat and shut his eyes. He had the ability to sleep anytime, anywhere. Within a minute or two, he was out. His mouth crept open as he slept, and Daisy, peaking over at him from her book, gently pushed his jaw up to shut it. Daisy put her tablet down and stared out the window. With the sun being up, there was more to see. She marveled at the colors. They were different than the ones at home. The greens were greener and the reds redder. Even the sun seemed sunnier. It really was paradise. The driver rounded a turn a little quicker than usual, and Duke stirred. Daisy was able to see down the side of the volcano.

"Beautiful."

"What is?"

Duke spoke with his eyes still shut.

"Look down the side."

He opened his eyes and then blinked a couple of times and looked out the window. The driver started speaking.

"If you look out the window to your left, you can see the lava flow. Hileakila last erupted about 150 years ago, and you can see the path the lava took. When you are in the middle of the path as we will be soon, you don't really notice it, but if you are at the top looking down or on the bottom looking up, it is very clear."

"Well, that's neat."

'Yes, it is. So, what are we going to do when we get back?"

"The first thing is eat some breakfast."

"Of course, it is."

"Hey, a man's got to eat."

"I want to go for a walk after breakfast."

"Sounds good to me. I'm going to need to walk around after eight hours on the bus."

"Yeah, and tomorrow is a beach day and then Friday, it will be another day on the shuttle."

"What's that thing we are doing on Friday/"

"The Road to Hana."

"That's right. The Road to Hana."

Two seats behind them, Peter Smith with his Nosy Neighbor was listening to every word.

Chapter 52

Once he was back at the resort, Peter Smith called Candace and shared the agenda of the Missouri couple with her.

"They should be alright here for the next couple days. But just to be safe, why don't you and Duber stay here at the resort and keep an eye on them."

"What will you be doing?"

"I'll be preparing a surprise for our friends along the Road to Hana."

"We'll be right over."

Chapter 53

Arbackle was not looking forward to the phone call from Moscow. By this time, he had hoped to have all his business in Hawaii wrapped up, but he was no better off than he was before he got there. Peter Smith was still alive, the deal with Criscoe Oila was on hold, and he hadn't paid the mole from the Shop. It wasn't supposed to be this hard.

The phone rang. Arbackle inhaled deeply and then quickly exhaled.

"Hello."

"Hello, Fatty."

"Um, how's everything in Moscow."

"It's raining. Did you finally succeed?"

"Well, no, not exactly."

"What do you mean?"

"Well, he's not exactly dead."

"So, is he in a coma, on life support? What do you mean not exactly?"

'Well, about now he's probably napping. It was quite a morning."

"So, you failed completely."

"Listen, we took our shots at the top of the volcano. I'm still half blind, and Dmitri nearly had his head knocked off. Peter Smith is no slouch."

"You said you could handle this?"

"I can. I will. But I might need a little more…"

"A little more what?"

"Well, I think our mole might help us identify his weakness, but we kind of owe him some money."

"You want more money? Who did you think we

are—the KGB?"

"Once we get everything flowing through the Philippines, we will be swimming in cash."

"No more money until Peter Smith is dead. And no more time. You have until the end of the week to get this done, or we're pulling the plug."

"Understood."

The Russian put his phone down. A few seconds later it rang again. He picked it up quickly.

"Hello."

Criscoe Oila laughed into his ear.

"Hey, Fatty, I love the plan. So, when do I get my money?"

"Soon. You'll get it soon."

"I hope so. It's a good plan. I'd hate to go into business with someone else."

"What are you saying?"

"I like you, Fatty. But if you can't come through on your end, I will find somebody who can."

"But it's my plan."

"And it's a good one, but business is business."

Arbackle hung up, but the phone rang again.

"Hello."

"Uh, hello?"

"Oh, it's you. I mean, it's you, just the person I wanted to talk to."

"Good. Because I still haven't gotten my money."

"What? They haven't paid you? It must be a bookkeeping error. I'm sure…"

"I have risked everything here. I have exposed our best agent, and I expect to be paid."

"Of course, you do. I'm just sick about the whole thing. If you weren't so far away, I'd pay you out of my own pocket."

"That will work."

"What?"

"I'll come to you. Where are you?"

"I'm on Maui, but you don't need to come all the way down here."

"It's no problem. I've always wanted to see a hula girl in person."

"But…"

"I'll book a flight for tomorrow. Aloha."

"Yeah, aloha."

Arbackle put his phone down. He had really stepped in it now.

Chapter 54

Winston Salem began working at the Shop in Research. He was the investigator who kept tabs on the Pit and noted who their recruits were and who was a rising star. He kept a white board that was visible to everyone who walked by his office. Written on the white board were what appeared to be the code names of Pit agents, and each had a colored star next to his name. No one knew who the agents were by their code names nor did they know the meaning of the stars, but that didn't stop the staff of the Shop from being captivated by it all. No one ever asked Salem what it all meant, and he never said. There was quite the drama involved with the stars. Lunch time discussions would be about the rise and fall of agents by their stars.

"Did you see that Buttercup is now a green. He'll be a red star before you know it."

"Can you believe that Tenderizer is now a silver. I thought Hot-to-Trot would be a silver first."

Many were greatly impressed with the white board, and they all agreed that Winston Salem was a genius. What they didn't know is that the white board wasn't about Pit agents. He was evaluating the female staff at the Shop based on their desirability. Salem was pleased that so many of the staff were curious about the white board because it served as a distraction from the actual research he was doing. He was studying those around him and learning their secrets, so he could sell them out. He was also researching who at the Pit would be best to approach to sell that information. One Pit agent stood out above the rest—Feyodor Fatty Arbackle. He gathered as much information as he could on the Junior Arbackle. He was ambitious and well connected. He seemed like someone who could be approached.

Salem initiated the relationship through the mail. He sent the Russian agent a 20% coupon to the Buffet Barn with a short note. "There's more where that came from."

A few days later, he sent a coupon from Sir Sydney's Shop for the Big Man—buy a coat and pair a pants and get another pair free. There was another note. "I have information about where to SHOP."

The third mailing included an ad he cut out from Everything Phoney for a bulk rate on burn phones. It included his last note. "Call for more SHOPPING information."

It included the number to one of his burn phones. Then he waited.
Several days went by with no response. Salem didn't worry. He knew Arbackle would be intrigued, and it was only a matter of time before he called.

Salem was sitting on a bench in Wolf Creek Park on a Saturday harassing the women that went by when the phone finally rang. He smiled and answered it.

"Hello Mr. Arbackle."

"Who is this?"

"You can call me Pomme de terre."

"Pomme de terre? That's French for potato. You want me to call you "potato?"

"The name isn't important. I have shopping information for you."

"Yeah, I got your messages. Listen, I don't know what you are selling, but I'm not buying."

"I'm selling information about shopping."

"Uh huh."

"Shopping information, you know, information about the Shop."

"The Shop?"

"Yes, the Shop."

"Oh, the Shop. Well, why didn't you say so."

"I sent you those cryptic messages. I thought you would figure it out."

"Nope. I just thought you were trying to sell me life insurance or something. So, what do you want?"

"I'm a well-placed operative at the Shop, and I'm prepared to provide you and the Pit some useful information for a price."

"What kind of information?"

"What do you want to know?"

"How do I know I can trust you? I don't want to end up on one of those TV shows where they pull practical jokes. What's it called—Puked?"

"Punked. I'm not from that show."

"OK, so how do I know you are who you say you are and that I can trust you."

"How about I give you a freebee to start. I'll text you some damaging information about one of our division chiefs, and you do with it as you please. If you like the results, we'll be in business together."

"OK."

"I'll be in touch soon."

Two days later Arbackle received a text. "William Harmonica—Linguistics—Visits the Smithsonian every day on his lunch hour and steals something."

115

Arbackle didn't reply, but he did place an anonymous phone call to the museum. Two days later, he received a text. It was a link to a bizarre story from the Washington Post about a man who was arrested for stealing from the Smithsonian Museums. When they searched his house, investigators discovered several items including a tie worn by Clark Gable in Gone with the Wind, a bone from a velociraptor and a moon rock.

The administrators of the Pit were excited about the possibility of having a mole. They decided to use him immediately to help them eliminate their chief nemesis— super agent Peter Smith. Since the mole originally made contact with Arbackle, he was promoted to agent and given the task of eliminating Peter Smith. He relished the opportunity. He would kill Peter Smith and then have free reign to implement his plan for an international heroin pipeline. He asked Mr. Potato for the file on Peter Smith. Winston Salem provided that information, but he was never paid. He decided to go to Maui to get the money himself.

Chapter 55

After Duke and Daisy finished eating lunch, they began walking around the grounds of the resort. There were different plants and trees full of colors and smells. The resort had several groundskeepers working outside, and Duber, having borrowed one of their uniforms, was able to keep close to the couple without being noticed. They took photos of all the different flora and fauna and made plans to move to the island as soon as they won the lottery.

They came upon a wedding that was taking place on the grounds. There were several guests sitting in white chairs. The bride and groom were in front preparing to say their vows. The bride wore a sleeveless white sundress. Her maids wore sundresses that were very similar to hers only they were yellow. The groom and his men all wore matching Hawaiian shirts and khakis. No one wore any shoes.

Daisy smiled.

"We should renew our vows sometime."

"We don't need to. The first time seems to have worked out just fine. Let's not tempt fate."

Duke grabbed Daisy's hand, and they walked back to their room.

Chapter 56

Thursday was beach day for Daisy and Duke, or at least it started out that way. There was restricted access to the beach, and to get there, they had to go past the pool and walk about 300 feet along a narrow path. Candace was seated on a lawn chair by the pool. She could see everyone that would come and go to the beach.

When the couple reached the sand, Duke took off his shoes and ran a few steps. It was somewhere around the third or fourth step when he realized he had made a terrible mistake. The sand was hot. Very hot. Burning hot. For a moment he thought it was the end. He saw himself losing his balance and falling into the sand where his body would melt within seconds. How could he escape? He turned around and headed out of the sand. One step and then another and another. He was so close. One more step and a leap, and he was there. He sat down on the grassy path and slowly and carefully put his shoes on his feet.

Daisy, who was well shod, called out to him.

"Are you coming?"

"Go on. I'll catch up."

Daisy found a spot on the beach and put her things down. Duke tentatively made his way to the spot and joined her. He gingerly placed his towel on the sand and lowered himself on top of it. Once he was down, he noticed how hard the wind was blowing.

"What do you think?" Daisy asked.

Duke couldn't hear her over the wind.

"What?"

"What do you think…about the beach?"

"It's different."

"The sand is really hot."

"What?"

"The sand is hot."

"I know."

"The wind is really blowing."

"What? I can't hear you over the wind."

"Let's go in the water."

"OK."

They walked towards the ocean. Once they reached the wet, cooler sand, they took off their shoes and left them on the beach.

"Do you think they will be all right there?"

Duke looked up and down the empty beach.

"I don't think anyone will steal them."

"No, do you think they will get washed away?"

"I don't plan on being in the water long enough for the tide to come in that much."

They got in the water up to their knees and walked along the surf. Daisy would occasionally glance back at their shoes.

"Do you see any shells?"

"Nope."

"It's really beautiful here."

"Yes."

"Do you want to go sit by the pool?"

"Yes!"

The couple walked back to their shoes and put them on. Then they gathered up their things from the beach and headed toward the pool.

Even though she could see the entrance to the

beach access and knew they were safe, Candace was relieved to have Daisy and Duke back in her sight. They made their way around the pool and found the only two vacant chairs that were together, and they just happened to be right next to Candace.

She closed her eyes as the couple put their things down. Before Duke sat down, he asked Daisy if she would like some lemonade.

"Oh, that would be great."

"OK, I'll be right back."

Duke walked over to a drink stand. Daisy sat back on the chair and relaxed. Candace opened her eyes briefly just as Daisy looked her way.

"It's nice here."

Candace froze for just a second. Her job was to observe, and if necessary, protect. That usually didn't include making small talk, but she tried.

"It is."

"We were out on the beach. The wind was terrible."

Candace nodded.

"But it's nice here at the pool."

"Yes."

"Are you getting married?"

"What? No"

"It seems like every young girl here is getting married. The waiter said they had 20 weddings booked this week."

"Really?"

"Yes. We had our big day 25 years ago at the courthouse. It wasn't exactly Hawaii."

"You should renew your vows here."

"No, Duke…He made all the arrangements right down to the very last detail. Although he did sort of screw up the flight. Our seats weren't next to each other on the plane. He took somebody else's seat, and fortunately he never showed up. So, I guess the people on the plane assumed Duke was that man."

Candace's eyes got big. She had figured it out.

"So, that's why…"

Daisy looked over to her.

"Um… I think I know why Duke didn't make plans to renew your vows."

"Oh?"

"He probably didn't know how important it was to you."

"I suppose you're right."

Duke walked up with the lemonade.

"Here you go. I told the guy to give the lemon a little extra squeeze, just for you."

"Thanks. I was just telling her about our wedding."

"Did you tell her about Johnny Boy Sims? Alligator love and crocodile kisses…"

The couple told Candace all about the concert. They sat by the pool for about two hours and then decided to go up to their room. Candace secretly followed them to the elevator. Just as the door closed, she turned around, and standing in front of her was someone she hadn't expected to see.

Chapter 57

When Winston Salem was purchasing his airline ticket from the online travel agency, he saw a good deal at a resort to pair it with. That resort was the Isle of Lahaina. He summoned Arbackle to the airport to pick him up. He and Dmitri were waiting at baggage claim when Salem walked up.

"Fatty batty."

"Mr. Potato?"

"Call me Pomme de terre."

"How did you recognize me?"

Salem looked Arbackle up and down and laughed, perhaps louder and longer than was necessary.

"Are you kidding me? I'd recognize you anywhere. Besides, I've studied your file. Who's the little fellow?"

"That's Dmitri."

"Great, now everybody knows everybody. Come on, I've got my luggage right here. Let's go."

The three walked to Dmitri's car. Salem sat in the back seat and spoke to those in the front.

"I'm staying at a place called the Isle of Lahaina. Are you familiar with it?"

"Yes. That's where Peter Smith is staying."

"Peter Smith? You mean you still haven't killed him? Dad can't be happy."

"We're working on it."

"So, where's my money?"

"Well, that's a problem. My bosses at the Pit are holding up payment until Peter Smith is dead."

"That's not my problem. I gave you his file now I

want my money."

"Yeah, well, I don't have it, and I won't have it until Peter Smith is dead."

"So, what am I supposed to do, help you kill him."

"Yeah, that would be great."

"You're unbelievable."

"He practically blinded me, and he knocked Dmitri out."

Dmitri nodded and rubbed his head.

"We need more information. We need to know his weakness."

"Everybody knows what his weakness is. He likes the girls. And they like him. You should have some Russian gal as your partner instead of Dmitri. Then he would come to you."

Dmitri turned around and sneered at him.

"He's traveling with a woman. They are playing man and wife."

"I bet they are."

"Anything you can think of will be helpful. It's in your interest as much as ours."

Dmitri parked the car at the Isle of Lahaina. Salem checked in at the front desk. As they were heading to the elevator, Salem saw Candace.

"Well, look at that, boys, it's my little handy dandy Candy Kane."

Winston Salem grabbed her by the arm.

"It looks like I have a date tonight…Easy, girl, don't make a scene."

They walked to the elevator. The door opened, and Duber was getting off. His eyes met Candace's, and she gave a quick shake of her head and got on the elevator with the men.

The Russians took Candace up to Salem's room.

"Who's she?" Arbackle asked.

"Boys, meet Candy Kane. How would you like to find her in your stocking at Christmas?"

He stroked her arm, and she jerked it away.

"Do you have any rope?"

Dmitri made exaggerated movements as if he her were searching for rope on his body. Arbackle sighed.

"We don't have any rope."

"What kind of spies are you? No wonder you lost the cold war."

He looked around the room and then down at their sneakers.

"I have an idea. Fatty, take your shoes off."

Dmitri spoke up. "You don't want him to do that." He shook his head and held his nose.

"Take your shoes off and give me your laces."

"How am I going to keep my shoes on?"

"You'll figure it out."

Arbackle did as he was told. Dmitri and Salem winced at the smell. Arbackle took out the shoelaces and gave them to Salem.

"Lay face down on the bed."

Candace did as she was instructed. Salem tied her hands behind her back with one lace and her feet with the other. Then he turned her over and sat her up on the bed.

"Comfy?"

"Traitor!"

"Now, now, there's no need for name calling. Besides, I see myself more as an entrepreneur. Now, Candy, we need some information."

"I'm not going to tell you anything."

"Don't be like that. We need you to tell us what we want to know. Between the three of us, we can do many unpleasant things, and even a few pleasant ones."

He lay next to her and stroked a strand of her hair. Candace glared at him.

"Where's Peter Smith?"

"I don't know."

"Now, Candy, don't make me get rough with you."

"I don't know. He didn't tell me where he was going."

"What's he doing here?"

"He found out someone wanted to kill him. He was trying to find out who."

"Is he working alone?"

Arbackle spoke up.

"No, he's working with another woman."

"Really, who is she, Candy?"

"She's an actress. When he found out someone was trying to kill him, he hired her to pose as his wife."

"They are very believable, too. If I didn't know better, I would swear they were just tourists."

"Interesting. So, what's he up to."

"He was contacted by someone who said he had information for him. He's meeting him tomorrow. They are going to connect somewhere along the road to Hana. He doesn't know where."

"How's he getting to Hana?"

"They are taking a shuttle from here, you know, like tourists."

Salem got up from the bed.

"OK, boys, there you have it. Find out what time the shuttle leaves tomorrow and follow it."

"Aren't you coming with us?"

"I can't. Peter Smith will recognize me. Besides, somebody needs to stay here and look after our little handy dandy Candy Kane."

He smiled and opened the door.

"Kill Peter Smith and get me my money."

The Russians left. Salem closed the door and locked it. Then he licked his lips and headed toward the bed and Candace.

Chapter 58

Duber was panicking. The bad guys had Candace. He didn't know where she was and what they were doing to her. He wanted to go bang on every door in the resort and try to find her. He needed to do something. He didn't know where Peter Smith was and had no way to contact him. He went up to the room and paced. He walked onto the balcony. He could hear Daisy and Duke talking below him. At least they were safe. He paced and cursed himself. He should have done something even though Candace obviously didn't want him doing anything. Maybe it would be alright. Candace was smart. She was resourceful. She could definitely take care of herself. But there were three of them and only one of her.

There was a knock on the door. Duber grabbed one of the knives. There was a second knock, and then the knob turned, and the door opened.

"Housekeeping."

Duber exhaled and put the knife away.

"Hello."

The woman looked at him strangely.

"What are you doing here?

"This…this is my room."

"This is not your room. This is the handsome man's room. He is very handsome. Where is the handsome man?"

"I work with the handsome man. He told me to wait for him here."

"Are you sure you work with the handsome man?"

"I work with the handsome man and the beautiful

woman."

"I don't know any beautiful woman. I only know the handsome man." She smiled. "He is very handsome."

She was suspicious of Duber, and he needed to think of something quick. What would Peter Smith do? He glanced at her nametag.

"Are you Marda?"

She looked at him and was obviously somewhat confused.

"Yes, I'm Marda."

"Good. I have a message for you from the handsome man. He said 'Tell Marda I'm sorry I missed her, but I will have something special for her next time."

Marda's suspicion immediately changed to delight.

"The handsome man will have something special for me. Something special from the handsome man. You tell the handsome man I'll be back tomorrow for something special."

"I will tell him. Thank you, Marda,"

The housekeeper left.

Chapter 59

Winston Salem sized up his prey.

"I have a feeling we're both going to enjoy his."

Salem took his shirt off. Candace spoke.

"Wait, can I say something first?"

Salem looked down at her.

"Sure, sweetheart."

"I don't believe this is going to turn out like you think. In fact, I'm certain one of us is going to be very disappointed."

Salem took off his pants. Candace continued.

"You see, you have an exaggerated sense of yourself. You are not particularly smart or handsome."

"Well, that's not a very nice thing to say."

Salem lay on the bed next to her. Candace lowered her tone.

"You think you are clever, but you're not. You think you are a great spy, but you're not."

Salem started kissing her.

"I'm sure you think you're great in bed, but you're probably not, but I'll never know."

"Why would you say that?"

"Because you're also not very good at tying knots."

Candace took her hands out from behind her back. They were no longer tied together, and she slammed them against his ears. Salem put his arms around his head in pain. Candace rolled over and out of bed. Her feet were still tied, so she hopped over to the front of the bed and grabbed his suitcase and hopped over to him and hit him with it. She hopped and then hit, hopped and then hit. He was laying on the bed in obvious pain and shielding himself with his arms. She quickly untied the shoelace around her feet and tied Salem's hands behind his back. The other shoelace was still around one of her wrists. She tied his feet together with it. Then she went through his suitcase and found a pair of socks. She tied the ends of one of them together to create a gag and slipped it over his head and just before she put it over his mouth, she kissed him on the lips.

"By lover, you were great."

Then she put it over his mouth and tightened it. She grabbed the key to the room, and before leaving, she took the "Do not disturb" sign and put it on the outside of the door. She headed back to Peter Smith's room.

Chapter 60

Duber got a glass of water and took a gulp when he heard someone at the door again. There was no knock. The knob turned, and the door opened. Duber reacted without thinking. The glass in his hand was half full and when the door opened, he flung the water at it. He ducked and scurried across the room. Then he heard Candace's voice.

"Well, that's not the kind of welcome I was expecting."

Duber was both embarrassed and relieved. He grabbed a paper towel to dry her off. But she stopped him.

"What are you doing? I'm not a puppy who's been left out in the rain."

Duber looked at the marks on her wrists.

"Don't worry about that. The price of doing business. Besides I let them tie me up."

"What?"

"Listen, there is nothing more dangerous than a stupid man, and I was in the company of three stupid men. So, I had to take control of the situation by making them think they were in control. Do you get it?"

"No."

"The new guy. He works for the Shop, and he's a pig. He sees women as frail creatures who are basically helpless. I let him tie me up because I knew he would overestimate himself and underestimate me. I knew I could get out. I also knew he wouldn't try any funny business with the other two around because he respects his own privacy. So, I went along and made them believe they were forcing answers out of me when I was feeding them the information I wanted them to have. Then when the other two left, I let him know who was really in charge."

"What did you do?

"Let's just say, my knots are stronger than his. We'll have to check on him in a bit."

"You're amazing."

"Don't let it get out. So, let's talk about tomorrow. The Russians are planning on killing the couple from Missouri along the Road to Hana."

"Why?

"The Russians think the man is Peter Smith."

"Really?"

"Yes, so you and Peter are going to have to stop them."

"What about you?"

"I have to stay here with Mr. Wonderful upstairs."

"OK, but there is just one problem."

"What's that?"

"I don't really know Peter Smith."

"What do you mean?"

"I don't know what he looks like. I've never seen him in person."

"I guess you haven't. Well, that makes things interesting,"

"How will I know him?"

"I guess you won't. But he'll know you. You'll just have to wait until he makes contact. Until then, keep an eye on the couple from Missouri."

"Got it."

Chapter 61

Peter Smith walked into the office of Maui Primo Tours. There was a woman working at a desk, and she greeted him as he walked up to her.

"Well, hello."

"Is this where I catch the shuttle?"

"Um, no, this is just where we take the reservations. The driver will pick you up at your hotel."

"Well, I guess I muffed that up. Oh well. But not all is lost."

He smiled and held out his hand.

"I'm Xavier."

"I'm Holly. Holly Jolly."

She extended her hand. Peter Smith grabbed it and held onto it a little too long.

"Well, Holly Jolly, I wonder if you could take me on a tour."

"Where do you want to go?"

"Wherever you want to take me."

Chapter 62

Daisy and Duke walked to the shuttle stop. There were four other tourists already there. Duke spoke.

"Are you going to Hana?"

"Yes, we are."

Daisy joined in.

"Have you ever been?"

"No, it should be great."

"It will be a beautiful day for a ride."

The shuttle pulled up, and the tourists got in. A final passenger walked out of the shadows and onto the shuttle. It was Duber. The shuttle had already picked up passengers from the other resorts, and it was nearly full. Daisy and Duke took a seat near the back. Duber took the seat behind them. As the shuttle began pulling away, the driver started speaking.

"Welcome to Maui Waui Island Tours, and wow wee do we have a great trip for you today as we take the Road to Hana. We'll be travelling on routes 36 and 360, but most people call it the Road to Hana or the Hana Highway. Now, some of you may ask what's in Hana that makes it such a sought-after attraction." One of the passengers took the bait.

"Yeah, what's in Hana?"

A few passengers laughed.

"I'm glad you asked. The answer is nothing. That's right—nothing. There really isn't anything in Hana that you wouldn't see in any small town. On this trip the journey really is more important than the destination. We will be traveling about 60 miles on our way to Hana, and much of it will be through a lush rain forest. There are more than 600 curves along the way, and we will cross more than 50 bridges. In several spots the road will be reduced to just one lane, so we will be traveling very slowly, and we will make several stops for numerous waterfalls, caves, beaches and more. Other sites of interest include the Garden of Eden and the Old Stone Church. Keep the cameras on your phones ready because there will photo opportunities around every curve."

Chapter 63

Arbackle and Dmitri began following the shuttle as it departed the resort. The mood in the car was not pleasant. They were desperate. Moscow wouldn't accept another failure. They were also still feeling the humiliation of what happened on top of the volcano. Neither told the other what really happened, but both were upset that he defeated them with so little effort. What made him so clever is that he appeared not to be clever at all. They talked about what lay ahead of them.

"So, where are we going today?"

"We're taking the Road to Hana."

"What's in Hana? Disneyland?"

"What, there is no Disneyland in Hawaii."

"Too bad. I've never been to Disneyland."

"People drive to Hana to see all the beautiful natural sights."

"Like what."

"Waterfalls."

"Waterfalls? What's the big deal? Water starts up here and goes down there and creates a waterfall in process. It's what water does. Back in St. Petersburg, pipes get holes in them all the time and leak down and create waterfall. No one comes to see that."

"This is different. It's natural."

"Waterfalls-- no big deal."

"So, anyway, we should work together this time."

"Is it cold on the Road to Hana."

"No."

"Then we will work together."

"They have seen me more than once. I need to keep a low profile."

"You…a low profile…That's a good one, Fatty."

"So, they will be making several stops along the way. We are going to have to play it by ear and take the opportunity when it comes."

"OK, Fatty."

Chapter 64

The shuttle arrived at its first destination.

"The first stop on our trip today is Twins Falls. This is somewhat misnamed. There are two main waterfalls, and they are similar, but they are not identical. I suppose they could be fraternal twin falls."

No one laughed, so he continued.

"There are also several other, smaller falls along the path. You could say there are many mini waterfalls. We'll stop here for a few minutes and give you a chance to walk along the path and take a few photos."

The shuttle pulled to a stop. There were a few cars in the parking lot and along with the Maui Waui shuttle, there was one from Maui Tours Dot Com and Maui Primo Tours. The tourists got out and walked along the path.

Daisy and Duke joined the other tourists. They marveled at the beauty of the falls and took several photos. Duber was part of the crowd, but he was not really looking at the waterfalls. He was looking at the crowd for someone menacing. He was also trying to spot Peter Smith.

Arbackle and Dmitri got out and began walking along the path, but after a few steps, one of Arbackle's shoes fell off.

"Ugh, this isn't going to work. There are too many people around them, and I just lost a shoe."

"You should have gotten more laces."

"Thanks. You're a big help. We'll find a place down the road."

138

The Russians returned to their car.

After the tourists had seen enough of the falls, they too returned to their respective cars and shuttles. Once all the passengers had returned to the Waui Maui shuttle, the driver headed down the road. The shuttle moved slowly from point to point. This was perfectly fine for the tourists as it gave them ample time to take more photos, but not so much for the Russians who just wanted to accomplish their mission and move on.

As the shuttle approached the Garden of Eden, the driver began speaking.

"Our next stop on the tour is the Garden of Eden. There are 26 acres of trails through some of the most beautiful plant life you will ever see. Many of the plants are exclusive to Hawaii. Your senses will be filled with brilliant colors and amazing scents. Some have said it has an almost hypnotic effect of them. Enjoy."

The tourists unloaded from the shuttle. Other tourists from other shuttles also arrived. The Russians stuck close to the Maui Waui shuttle and followed the tourists while keeping a safe distance. The tourists began to break up into small units.

"This looks like the place. Everyone is spreading out."

"Yeah."

Dmitri started giggling.

"What's so funny?"

"Can you smell that?"

"What? Oh, the plants. Yes, it's very nice."

"Hey, Fatty, you're not such a bad guy."

His giggling continued.

"Um, thanks."

"No, I mean it. I don't care what anybody else says. You're a good guy."

"Are you alright?"

Dmitri inhaled deeply.

"Yeah."

The giggling was almost out of control.

"What's wrong with you?"

"Did you see…the Wizard of Oz?"

"Yeah, everybody has seen it. Why?"

"Do you remember the pop…pies, poppies…"

He lay down on the ground and stared up at the sky. Arbackle looked down at him.

"Are you high?"

"Hey, Fatty, I don't think I can kill anybody right now?"

"I can see that."

"I can kill them, later."

"OK. Get up."

"I can't."

Arbackle pulled him up. Dmitri started looking around in amazement.

"Look at the colors—all the greens and yellows and reds. Oh, there's some blue. I like blue. Hey, Fatty, I like blue. I like blue very much."

"Great, I like blue, too. Now, let's get you back to the car."

The Russians retreated to their car, so Dmitri could recover from the sensory overload.

Duber, who had spotted the Russians shortly after getting off the shuttle, smiled and shook his head as he witnessed Dmitri's overdose on nature.

Duke and Daisy explored the Garden of Eden.

They took many phots and found themselves separated from the crowd many times. Both agreed they had found paradise in paradise.

Chapter 65

The tour continued though the rain forest along the Road to Hana. They saw the Upper Waikani Falls and the Hanawai Falls. The tourists continued to be amazed at the beauty around them. Dmitri continued to be less than impressed, and Arbackle continued to have problems with his shoes. When they came to the Kahanu Garden, the Russians stayed in the car so as not to have a repeat of their previous garden experience. They were running out of opportunities along the road. They would have to act soon. They decided to be proactive. They drove ahead to stake out a good place for a killing. They came to a black sand beach.

"Hey, Fatty, the sand is black."

"I see that."

"Why is it black?"

"I don't know. Exon?"

Dmitri bent down and took a handful and examined it closely. Then he smelled it?

"What's it smell like?"

"It doesn't smell like Exon. It smells like sand."

He released it and brushed it from his hand.

"This is very weird."

"Let's go. There's a cave up here that might be perfect for our needs."

They walked to the Wai'anapanapa cave. A sign explained the legend associated with the cave.

"Hey, did you see this? A Hawaiian princess ran away from her husband and hid here. He found her and killed her."

"Too bad for her."

"Now, on the anniversary of her death, the pool in the cave turns red."

"Is the cave haunted?"

"No, it's not haunted."

"It sounds haunted."

"Well, maybe it's a little bit haunted."

The Russians went into the cave. They found a remote spot.

"This will be perfect. We'll lure him down here, and…"

"Zzzzz."

"Yeah, zzzzz."

Dmitri took out a knife.

"Try not to lose this one. Knives don't grow on trees, you know…Shh, did you hear something?"

"No."

"There it is again."

It was a man's voice.

"Popo'alaea…Popo'alaea…I will find you…You can't leave me… Popo'alaea. I will kill you…And everyone in this cave."

Arbackle turned around to flee and ran into Dmitri knocking his knife out of his hand. The Russians began running back to where they entered the cave. Arbackle got a few steps before he lost his shoe. He picked it up and continued running. After a few more steps, he lost the other shoe. He picked it up and ran barefoot out of the cave.

After the Russians were gone, Peter Smith wearing a Maui Primo Tours shirt emerged from the darkness.

Chapter 66

Peter Smith had a lovely time with Holly Jolly, and while she had certain irresistible charms, he was mostly interested in her shuttle. After she gave him a tour of some places most visitors never see, he slipped away with her shirt and her keys, and he took the van along the Road to Hana.

He had been shadowing the Russians since Twin Falls. He blended in with the other tour drivers, and no one noticed that he didn't have any passengers. He slipped into the cave and heard the Russians plotting, and then he decided to have a little fun at their expense. After they scurried out, he saw the knife that Dmitri had dropped. "This might come in handy," he said, and he picked it up and put it in his pocket. He returned to his shuttle and looked around for the Russians, but they were nowhere to be seen. He headed toward Hana certain he would see them soon.

Chapter 67

The tourists continued on the Road to Hana. Duke and Daisy strolled along the black sand beaches and explored the caves which it would seem were not haunted at all. They explored ancient Hawaiian ruins and navigated a bamboo forest. One of their last stops was what the locals called "the Old Stone Church." It was built on one of the highest points of Maui in the 19th century and was the only structure on the east coast of Maui to survive a devastating tsunami in 1946. It was neither large nor elaborate. It was not adorned with any statues or ornaments. It was just a simple structure where one could come to pray or meditate. Its magnificence was in its very existence, that it had been spared when everything else had been washed to sea.

Daisy and Duke quietly entered the church. They spoke in respectful, hushed tones and snapped a few photos. They were alone in the church, but they were not alone. Duber remained outside looking for danger. But Duber also wasn't alone. A man behind him spoke.

"Keeping them safe?"

Duber turned around.

"Peter Smith, I presume."

"You presume correctly."

"They are in there alone, but I have a bad feeling."

"I have been watching the Russians most of the day, but I lost them after the caves. I thought they might make a move up here."

"I haven't seen them."

"Well, stay alert."
"I will."

Chapter 68

Peter Smith and Duber didn't know that their adversaries were indeed on the grounds of the church. They were along the edge of a cliff. To the average tourist, it would have been a fabulous view. One could see the bay and the remaining few miles left on the Road to Hana including a small stretch of road on a narrow isthmus that could be very dangerous to the inexperienced or distracted driver. A few inches off to the right or to the left could lead to a spill into the bay. The rocky shoreline would make a rescue unlikely. A sign leading up to that point of the road warned of the potential danger, but if the travelers were to complete their journey, it was the only option. The Russians knew the shuttle carrying Peter Smith would travel on that isthmus, and they had a terrible plan.

Chapter 69

Duber joined the rest of the tourists on the Maui Waui Shuttle as they began the final stretch on the Road to Hana. The driver prepared the passengers for the road ahead.

"Folks, we are approaching one of the trickier parts of the drive. The narrow roadway is the only path to Hana, so hold your breath and say your prayers."

The van started down the isthmus. There was water on both sides just a few feet below the road.

"You might want to do what I do and close your eyes."

There was muffled laughter from the crowd.

"Just kidding, of course. Some of the rental car companies won't let you have a car unless you promise not to make this drive. It's…what the heck!" The driver slowed down, and then started driving erratically as a bright flash of light shone on the shuttle. The blinding light came from a spot on a cliff above the highway. The driver turned his head to the left to avoid the blinding light, and when he did, his arms on the steering wheel followed. The van lunged forward and to the left. The front left wheel went off the roadway and over the side. The driver turned the wheels to the right and tapped the gas pedal trying to move forward. The van jerked to the right and then to the left. The rear tire was now off the road.

"Hey folks, we have a bit of problem here. Could everyone sitting on the left side of the shuttle slowly move over to the right side. This might be a good time to introduce yourselves to the people next to you as you are going to get mighty close."

The passengers on the left began moving quickly and squeezed next to the passengers on the right. In some cases, they sat on each other's lap. They were mostly quiet. The driver tried accelerating again. The van moved forward, but both the left wheels were still off the road.

"Well, it looks like you all are going to have a funny story to tell you grandkids."

The driver tried moving forward again. The wheels remained off the road.

Duber got up from his seat and walked to the front of the shuttle.

"Sir, I'm going to need you sit back down…"

"Where's the jack? The jack. Where's the jack?"

"It's in the back, but you don't understand, we don't have a flat…"

"I understand. Front wheel drive or rear wheel drive?"

"Eh… front wheel."

"Open the door."

"But you can't. There's no room."

"Open the door."

The driver did as he was told. There was less than a foot of pavement on the right side of the van. Duber clung to the van and inched himself toward the front. Once there, he climbed onto the hood and over the windshield, and on top of the van. The van wiggled as he got on top. He crawled to the back of the van and then slid off behind it. He opened the back and pulled up the false bottom to reveal the spare tire and the jack. He removed the jack and tire

iron and put them on top of the van. Then he got on
top of it and crawled back to front with the tools. He
tossed them off the van and then hopped off.

Duber got as close to the edge as he could, and
then he placed the jack underneath the van. Using the
tire iron, he began raising the left end of the van. He
raised it so the tire was now higher than the
pavement. He backed away from the van and
signaled the driver to turn his wheels to the right. The
driver followed his directions. Then he signaled for
him to hit the gas. The driver pressed the pedal and
the van moved slightly to the right and forward and off
the jack. The front tire was back on the pavement, but
now the van was at an awkward angle with the right
tire very close to the on the edge.
Duber picked up the jack and the tire iron and climbed
back on top of the van and made his way to the back.
He climbed down and placed the jack as close to the
edge as he could. Then he raised it up. When it was
high enough, Duber yelled to the driver.

"Listen to me carefully. On the count of three, I
want you to accelerate slightly and turn your wheel
quickly to the left. But go slowly or we will be right
back where we started or worse."

The driver accelerated and the van moved
forward and then to the left. The jack fell off and into
the water. All four wheels of the van were back on the
road. Duber looked toward the cliff, and the blinding
light was still flashing onto the windshield of the van.

"Don't move until that light disappears, but once it
does, go on to Hana."

"What about you?"

"Don't worry about me."

Duber started walking back to the Old Stone Church grounds. The Maui Primo shuttle driven by Peter Smith stopped in front of him.

"Get in. They're up by the church. Let's go."

They quickly drove to the church grounds and spotted Arbackle and Dmitri under a coconut tree along the edge of the cliff. They stopped the van, got out and snuck up on the Russians. Peter Smith was carrying the knife he had found earlier. He handed it to Duber and signaled for him to throw it into a trio of coconuts in the tree. Duber sent the knife flying, but he missed the coconuts, and the knife got stuck in the tree. He took out one of the knives he had retrieved from Dmitri and threw it. The result was the same. He had one knife left. He threw it, and this time he hit his target. The coconuts came falling out of the tree. One hit Arbackle on the head and another hit Dmitri. The third fell harmlessly to the ground. The Russians were both knocked out from the blow.
Peter Smith smiled.

"Did you know that more people are injured by coconuts than from sharks?"

"I didn't know that."

"It's true."

The rearview mirror from Dmitri's car was on the grass. They were using it to reflect the sunlight onto the van below. Duber looked down to the road. The van had started moving over the isthmus. After a few seconds, it had cleared the water and was on its way to Hana.

Peter Smith motioned towards the Russians.

"You check on them while I pull up the van."

The Russians were out cold, but they were

breathing.

Peter Smith and Duber loaded Dmitri into the van.

"Search Dmitri for some keys."

Duber found the keys to the car in his pocket. Then they rolled Arbackle onto the wheelchair lift and raised him into the van.

"I will drop you off at their car then follow me."

"OK."

Peter Smith drove to Hana and then back to town. He pulled into the parking lot of the Maui Prima Shuttles office. Dmitri was beginning to awaken, and Peter Smith pulled him into the driver's seat and then exited the van and got in the car with Duber.

Chapter 70

When Holly Jolly awoke, Xavier Carnahaha was gone along with her shuttle. She was very upset. Why would he just leave her like that after the night they spent together. She took a cab to work hoping he would return the van to her with a very good explanation along with some roses. After several hours, she reached the conclusion that something terrible had happened. She called the sheriff's office and reported a kidnapping.
When the deputies arrived, she told them about Xavier and the night they shared.

"And you think someone kidnapped Mr. Carnahaha and took your van?" asked the first deputy.

"It's the only explanation."

The second deputy was skeptical.

"Don't you think it's more likely…"

His partner cut him off.

"We'll file your report on the van, but don't get your hopes up."

"And a report on Xavier?"

"Oh yes, we'll file a report on him."

They were just wrapping up when they heard a car horn—HRRRRRRRRR. The three went out to investigate.

"That's my shuttle,"

They walked over to the van and found Dmitri inside with his head resting in the center of the steering wheel honking the horn. They found Arbackle behind him.

"Are either of these men Mr. Carnahaha?"

"No."

"Well, we'll take them in and get back to you."

Chapter 71

Despite having put out the "Do Not Disturb" sign, Candace felt a little funny about leaving Winston Salem alone in his room. So, she planned to spend most of her day up there with him.

"How are you doing, Winston honey? Do you need a change of socks?"

He just glared at her.

"Now, if you are a good boy, I will untie you and let you stretch a bit. But first, I am going to take a shower. Winston, I am going in there and taking off my clothes and take a shower. I will be totally naked, Winston, totally. But poor Winston will be stuck out here."

She blew him a kiss as she walked into the bathroom. She closed the door, but it didn't latch completely. She turned on the fan, started the water and got in.

The temptation was too great for Salem. He swung his legs to the side of the bed and hopped up. He stood there for several seconds while he got his balance then he started hopping. He hopped, regained his balance and then hopped again. He repeated this until he got to the bathroom door. He pushed it open with his head then he hopped into the bathroom. The humidity from the shower made the tile floor wet. He took a hop inside the bathroom and slipped, falling face down on the floor. Blood spilled from his nose.

Candace thought she heard something as she was showering, and she paused.

"Are you all right out there, Winston honey?"

She didn't hear anything except the fan. She continued showering. She washed her hair and then added the conditioner. Then she took a deep breath and turned off the water. She reached for a towel and dried herself off. Then she wrapped the towel around her and opened the shower curtain.

Candace shrieked and recoiled back into the tub when she saw Salem on the floor. She quickly composed herself and got out of the tub.

"What have you done, Winston?"

She turned him over and checked for a pulse. There was none. She removed the sock from his mouth and gave him mouth to mouth resuscitation. No luck. Then she tried pumping his chest. He still wasn't breathing. She repeated it all. After several minutes she stopped. Winston Salem was dead.

Candace untied his hands and feet. She got dressed and quickly left the room and went back to Peter Smith's room and waited.

Chapter 72

Candace was sitting outside on the balcony when she heard sounds coming from the room below. Daisy and Duke sat on their balcony and made plans for dinner. Candace was relieved to know they were OK. She assumed that both Duber and Peter Smith were also fine, but she would know for certain soon enough. About fifteen minutes later the door opened, and Peter Smith shouted,

"Honey, I'm home."

Candace came in from the balcony and smiled at Duber.

"I heard them downstairs a few minutes ago, so I guess everything was successful?"

"Very successful. I can't wait to tell you all about it. So, I hear you have been entertaining a guest?"

"Yes, Winston Salem came to visit. It turns out he was the traitor. He's upstairs. Would you like to see him?"

"Sure."

The three went to Salem's room. Candace unlocked the door, and they went in. Peter Smith looked around the room.

"Where is he?"

"Oh, he's in the bathroom."

Peter Smith went into the bathroom and then after a few seconds came out.

"Um, Candace, you have a dead traitor in your bathroom."

"It's not my bathroom."

"Well, um, that's not really the point."

"I didn't kill him. I was taking a shower, and he invited himself in. Then he slipped on the floor and cracked his skull. He really should have respected a woman's privacy."   "So, what were you planning on doing with him?"

"That's what I was asking myself all afternoon. 'What do you do with a dead traitor in the bathroom?'"

"Did you come up with any answers?"

"Well, the way I looked at it, no matter what I did, he was still going to be dead, and he was still going to be a traitor. That's as far as I got."

"What about you Duber?"

"Well, Candace is right. He is a dead traitor. But we probably shouldn't leave him for the maid to find."

"So, do you have any thoughts on how to get him out of here?"

"Sure. Throw him off the balcony."

Peter Smith and Candace looked at him for a few seconds without saying a word. Peter Smith spoke first.

"OK."

"Sounds good to me."

'OK, Duber, go through his pockets and take out his wallet and anything that would identify him. If you find any cash in there, you can keep it."

Duber cleaned out his pockets and found $200 in cash and his wallet. He pocketed the cash and gave the wallet to Peter Smith who was gathering up his belongings.

"OK, let's do it."

Peter Smith and Duber picked up Salem's body and carried him to the balcony.

"Wait a second. Put him down."

Peter Smith reached into his own wallet and took out something and put it into Winston Salem's pocket. Candace was curious.

"What's that?"

"A library card."

Candace and Duber looked at each other and shook their heads. The three picked up Salem's body. Peter Smith had his arms. Duber had his legs and Candace gave support in the middle.

"On three…One, two, threeeee."

Winston Salem's body went over the railing and landed on the ground eleven floors below. Peter Smith picked up Salem's bag, and the three left the room. He saw the opening to a garbage chute, opened it up and threw Salem's bag down. Then they went back to Peter Smith's room.

Chapter 73

"Well, what should we do now?" Peter Smith asked.

Candace had an idea.

"Can you charm your little concierge into doing a favor?"

"I can try. What do you have in mind?"

"A wedding."

"What? Listen, Candace, I like you, but..."

"Relax, it's not for you."

They both looked over at Duber.

"Um...I...Well..."

"It's not for you, either. Wow, there's nothing like the idea of a little marriage to turn two big manly spies into Jello. The wedding is for the folks downstairs. She wants to renew their vows, but he's too thick headed to notice."

"Well, I see spending the afternoon with a dead traitor in the bathroom hasn't taken away your romantic side."

"Go talk to your concierge."

Chapter 74

Peter Smith visited the concierge, Ella Mabella.

"Well, where have you been?"

"Working."

"Can I see you tonight?"

"Sadly, no. My sister and brother-in-law have stopped by."

Ella frowned at a couple who were extremely upset and talking to a manager.

"What's going on?" Peter Smith asked.

"They were planning on getting married here tomorrow, but tonight they were walking around the grounds when they came upon a dead body. They were quite distressed and concluded finding a dead body the night before their wedding was a bad omen and not the way to start off a marriage. They put off the wedding indefinitely. The manager is going to do whatever it takes to make them happy."

"Interesting. So, you have an opening for a wedding tomorrow."

"It would seem that way."

Peter Smith explained about wanting to arrange for Daisy and Duke to renew their vows, but he wanted Ella Mabella to surprise them with it.

"Tell them it was your idea. My sister will give you all the details."

Chapter 75

It was a busy time for the sheriff's department. Shortly after the deputies questioned the suspects in the stolen van, a call came in about a dead body at the Isle of Lahaina. The deputies investigated.

"Look at that. This man's face is so smashed in that his own mother wouldn't recognize him."

He had no wallet or ID, but then one of the deputies found something in his pocket. It was a library card. The name on it was Xavier Carnahaha. It seemed their two cases were related, and the men in custody had some explaining to do.

Chapter 76

Ella Mabella called the Duckworth's room.

"Hello, this is Duke."

"Hello Mr. Duckworth, This is Ella Mabella, the concierge.

"Yes."

"I'm calling to let you know that you and Mrs. Duckworth have been invited to a wedding tomorrow morning."

"Really, who's getting married?"

"Well, that's a secret right now."

'Is this some kind of trick? You're not going to try to sell us a timeshare. We've been tricked like that before."

"I promise, you will not want to miss this event."

"Well, this is very strange, but I will talk to my wife about it. Hey Daisy, the concierge has invited us to a wedding tomorrow?

"How nice. What time?"

"Well, I guess we're in. What time do you want us?"

"I will come by to get you at 9:45."

"We'll be ready."

Chapter 77

When Ella Mabella knocked on their door, the Duckworth's were ready for a wedding. Duke was wearing his finest Hawaiian shirt, and Daisy wore a bright green dress. Ella led them down to the garden area of the resort. They were met there by a young man.

"Daisy, Duke, my name is Donald Ho."

"Any relation?" Duke asked.

"Relation to whom?"

"Don...Don Ho."

"I'm sorry, I don't know who that is."

"Everybody knows Don Ho. Tiny Bubbles?"

Donald Ho shook his head.

"I'm an ordained minister who is employed here at the resort. Do you have any questions before we begin?"

"Yeah, who's getting married?"

"Well, you are, of course."

Duke was shocked, but Daisy was delighted.

"Oh Duke, you are the best. This is the greatest surprise ever."

Duke was torn between confessing that he had nothing to do with it and taking complete credit. He chose just to remain silent instead.

Donald Ho led them to the front of the garden area. A small crowd of employees and guests were in attendance. In the back sat Candace, Duber and Peter Smith.

Donald Ho addressed the congregation:

"Welcome, my friends. We come here today to

witness a renewal. Daisy and Duke were first joined in marriage 25 years ago, and they are here today to affirm their commitment to one another. I am certain that you have been through many challenges and difficult times that you never would have imagined 25 years ago. But here you are, through it all, still together and ready to start the next 25 years. Duke, do you once again take this woman to be your wife. To listen to her when she's talking, to let her have the good blanket. and to open cans and kill spiders."

"I do."

"Daisy, do you once again take this man to be your husband, to laugh at his jokes, to tolerate his snoring and to tell him when his clothes don't match?"

"I sure do."

"By the power vested in me by the state of Hawaii and the Isle of Lahaina Resort, I once again pronounce you man and wife. You may kiss the bride."

Duke and Daisy shared a kiss.

"Now, Daisy, Duke, along with being an ordained minister, I am also one of the entertainers here at the Isle of Lahaina, and I have a song I would like to sing that I understand is special to you."

Donald Ho picked up a guitar and began singing and playing.

"I went down to the bar just the other day.
I saw a little girl who was wantin' to play.
I said, "Hello, little momma, whadda say,"
She said, "Let's have fun the alligator way."
Alligator love and crocodile kisses,
Having us a time, just me and my misses.
Your dog gonna howl and you cat a hisses

At alligator love and crocodile kisses.

I said, "Now honey, I don't want to start a fight,
But them gators are mean, and they have a bad
bite.
They'll tear off your head with all of their might.
Alligator fun doesn't seem quite right.

She shook her said and said, "Listen, King Kong,
You think you're all right, but you're totally wrong.
Gators are smart and silent and strong,
And they can make love all night long."

Alligator love and crocodile kisses,
Having us a good time, just me and my misses.
Your dog gonna howl and you cat a hisses
At alligator love and crocodile kisses.

I haven't been the same since that day
When I learned how to love the alligator way.
I said, "Don't you ever leave; I want you to stay.
And we're still together, I'm happy to say.

Alligator love and crocodile kisses,
Having us a time, just me and my misses.
Your dog gonna howl and you cat a hisses
At alligator love and crocodile kisses.

Daisy and Duke sang along and danced to the
music. The crowd joined them. Later that night, they
returned to Missouri unbothered by spies and would-
be assassins and full of great memories.
    Peter Smith and Candace returned to Washington

and celebrated the newest member of the Shop team—Duber the Uber.

Winston Salem mysteriously disappeared and was never heard from again.

Feyodor Arbackle and Dmitri Pontiacivich stayed in Hawaii longer than they intended thanks to the state's criminal justice system.

The Shop and The Pit continued their covert affairs. The world remained unaware of their activities.

The End

Made in the USA
Monee, IL
09 September 2021